THE
RISE

DYSTOPIA

DAVID TOWNER

The sun set hours ago, and Haruki Sato hasn't seen daylight today.

Unless, of course, you count the dim glow between the slats of the window blinds. It is a hot day, summer making an early appearance. Haruki is grateful for the air conditioning. It's nearing midnight as Haruki glances at his watch, packing his bag hastily. If he doesn't hurry, he'll miss the last train.

Tokyo is a metropolis that never sleeps, but the business district of Marunouchi is void of any karaoke bars or maid cafes. Many windows of the surrounding skyscrapers, however, are illuminated. Businessmen and women are burning the midnight oil, showing their bosses how hard they work. Some, Haruki heard, miss the last train on purpose, either to avoid home life or go to a love hotel with someone else. Though Haruki isn't exactly desperate to return to his one-bedroom first floor apartment, he doesn't want to spend the night in the office either.

His papers now tucked safely in his leather messenger bag, he heads for the door, muttering "good work, everyone" to the few colleagues still at their computers. A supervisor, Mr. Nakamura, is slumped at his desk, arms folded, his head to the side and an odd look of peace on his face. Haruki quietly slips past him and finds the elevator, working out a crick in his back as he descends to the first floor. If he weren't so tired, he would head to the gym. His muscles always start to feel a little tight after a few days without exercise.

His thoughts float to Sakura, and he wishes they wouldn't. He saw on Instagram this morning that she is now engaged, a happy grin on her face as she showed off a sparkling engagement ring. The picture made him physically ill from jealousy, but it's his own fault for checking her social media in the first place. Like some creepy stalker.

Haruki grimaces and pushes Sakura from his mind. All he wants now is to crawl into his futon and sleep. Haruki likes his job, but he'll be glad when his latest project is over. The deadline is fast approaching and everyone in the office is feeling the pressure.

Haruki steps out of the building. It's a muggy May evening, his favorite season before the rainfall in June. With the dim glow of streetlamps and the quiet concrete street, it's unusually tranquil.

He steps off the stoop and water seeps into his shoe, instantly drenching his sock. He gasps then scowls. *Great.* He stepped right into a puddle. He didn't even know it rained today.

He looks down to avoid the puddle with his next step, but the water is unavoidable. The entire street is flooded. The grids on the streets struggle to absorb it all. Surprise ripples through Haruki as he glances around. What happened here? A leak?

He checks his watch again. Only eight minutes until the last train. Accepting his fate to have soggy socks for the entire forty-minute journey home, Haruki sprints to Tokyo Train Station.

He makes it just in time. He taps his travel card on the sensor with a familiar beep and hops onto the train, panting, a few seconds before the doors slide closed. Hoping he's not leaving wet footprints and that his suede shoes will survive the ordeal, he takes a seat in the mercifully quiet carriage as the train slides out of the station.

He glances to the next carriage, where an older man reads a newspaper, and a few young women giggle together. Have they noticed the weird water? Or was the leak just on his street?

Haruki glances outside as skyscrapers and department stores flash by. In the artificial lights, he spots more streets, and their lights reflect more water. Haruki swallows, concern creeping through him. If a river flooded or there was a sewage leak, it would only cover part of the city. But the water stretches for miles.

He takes out his phone and searches for an answer, curling his wet toes in his ruined shoes.

◆　◆　◆

"Ugh. Damn it."

The backpack is heavier than Andrea anticipated, but she carries it with the straps in the crook of her elbow, clenching her teeth as she half waddles to her car and wishing she at least had time for coffee. It should be illegal to be awake this early in the morning. She scowls at Lindsay's bedroom as she passes it, cursing whatever God there is for inventing six a.m.

At least the morning light is coming. The sun rises between some buildings, casting blinding orange light onto her, making her squint. Yawning behind her free hand, she heads to her car. The Rocky Mountains sit to the west, the morning sunlight bathing them in gold. Andrea has been in Boulder, Colorado for almost a year, and the sight still steals her breath away.

But it's the street that catches her eye this morning. Amid the neat, reddish buildings, water is cascading down the incline and into the sewer drain nearby. Andrea inhales through her nose, but there's no scent of sewage. At least that's something.

"Outstanding," she mutters sarcastically. She needs to get going. Rent is due soon. She clambers into her car and mounts her phone on its holder. She hastily pats her messy hair when she catches her reflection in the dark screen, then opens the

Rideshare app. Being a driver is a decent way to earn some cash on the side to get her through college. It beats working in a fast-food joint, anyway. People are much more polite when they're sitting in the back of your car. Usually.

She blinks and frowns at a nearby side street. For a moment, it looked like someone was peeking out at her from an alleyway. Her heart races.

Stop it, Andrea. There's no one there.

Her phone beeps with an offer for an airport transfer. Great! Hoping whatever's wrong with the street will be fixed soon, she drives along the wet street.

◆　◆　◆

"Callum, stop it! Your shoes are gonna get wet!" Stephanie's mom groans as five-year-old Callum jumps delightedly in some water, drenching his pants. "What the hell's happening here, anyway?" she adds to no one in particular, grabbing her son by the jacket.

The other people lining up to board the cruise ship are either complaining or having fun with the half-inch or so of water that has made its way into the ferry terminal. The enormous cruise ship awaits, its bright white hull and windows gleam in the spring sunshine. A few people have stepped up onto benches to avoid the water, muttering to each other about why no one has showed up to fix it.

"Probably a water main break or something," Stephanie's dad mutters, patting his pockets. He says a loud swear word and Callum giggles. "I'm going for a cigarette."

Stephanie watches her mom's face tighten, but she says nothing. She never says anything to Dad.

Stephanie watches her dad splash without care through a group of waiting people and out of sight. At least they'll be on board soon, and she'll be able to play her game in peace.

◆　◆　◆

Captain Spencer observes from the control room. As always before a trip, he feels anticipation mingled with guilt. He couldn't resist the call of the casino in Miami. He lost over six hundred dollars last night before finally managing to pry himself away from the blackjack table and make it back to the ship, guilt-ridden.

He kissed his wife goodbye yesterday afternoon and promised not to gamble, yet less than two hours later, there he was, playing again. He can't help it. The rush, the excitement, the high when he wins. He knows it's a problem, but whenever his wife suggests therapy, he insists he doesn't need it. And she doesn't even know how bad it really is.

Never mind, he tells himself, stroking his beard. *I can earn the money back. She doesn't need to know.*

His thoughts turn to the glimmering half-inch of water covering the Miami streets near the port. There must be a sewage overflow or water main break nearby.

Not his problem. Captain Spencer inhales, hoping the slight headache from the free casino whiskey will soon go away. As the passengers start to board, chatting and laughing together, the PA system crackles to life.

"Good morning, ladies and gentlemen," says Peter Swan, the cruise director. "We apologize for the soggy start to the morning. The city's still trying to track down the leak, but most likely by the time they find it, you'll be in Nassau enjoying a daiquiri."

Laughter ripples among the crowd and Captain Spencer smiles to himself. Swan always knows exactly what to say. "Our housekeeping staff has placed extra towels in every cabin, but please let us know if there's anything else we can do to make your morning more comfortable. We will be departing in approximately forty-five minutes."

◆ ◆ ◆

Haruki is startled awake. He immediately reaches for his iPhone to check the time. It's 5:55am. A bad dream has robbed him of twenty minutes of sleep once again. The Instagram app calls to him, but he resists looking. Stalking his ex-girlfriend won't make him feel any better.

News outlets are posting about the mysterious water. Speculation includes a tsunami or a leak, but it seems no one has been able to find the source. Haruki frowns. That doesn't sound right at all. Surely the authorities could have tracked it down by now.

He crawls out of his futon and passes his bookshelf, mostly full of his favorite manga comics, though there are several novels there, too. He glances outside. From here, he can't see much except the wall of the next apartment building. A dog barks somewhere as he leans out the window, an early morning breeze caressing his tousled hair as he looks down. Sure enough, the narrow alley is covered with water. From here, the water looks black.

Weird.

He shakes it off and heads to take a shower and get ready for work. If this water is widespread, it's likely that the subway will be flooded, so people will be scrambling for taxis. He should hurry. Twenty minutes later, his hair still damp, Haruki grabs an instant noodle pot from on top of his fridge and heads outside with his bag, suede shoes in one hand and flip flops on his feet. The water is ice cold and sure enough, black as tar.

He's lucky enough to flag down a cab, and the tires splash through the standing water as the driver navigates slowly toward their destination. Outside, there's hardly anyone around, and those who are out are wearing protective shoes or, like Haruki, flip flops. A little girl in wellington boots jumps and splashes water everywhere while her mother scolds her. Teenage boys laugh together as they ride their bicycles, leaving thin, temporary trails through the water. Trepidation runs through Haruki, but the project deadline is approaching. He can let the authorities worry about this strange water for now.

He sends a text to his younger brother, Tatsu, who lives back in Chiba. Haruki hesitates for a moment before asking him if they've heard about the water problem. Haruki can hear the smooth splashing sound of the taxi's tires going through the water. The sound reminds him of the rainy season.

"I don't know," comes his brother's reply a few moments later. *"Haven't been outside today."*

Haruki chews the inside of his cheek. On a Tuesday, his fourteen-year-old brother should be in school, but Tatsu hasn't bothered going for several months now. He says what's the point in studying just to become a boring businessman. He much prefers to sit in his room and watch movies and play video games.

What if Tatsu ends up a *hikikomori*, a social recluse who never goes outside? Haruki makes a mental note to visit his family as soon as he can. Maybe he can talk some sense into him. He looks out the window, thinking about the work deadline. Maybe he should have stayed later in the office last night and crashed in a capsule hotel or something. Although Haruki loves his job and he's been accused—by both his mother and his ex-girlfriend Sakura—of being a workaholic, he doesn't want to become one of those men whose whole life is his job.

Gym tonight, he decides, leaning back in the taxi and closing his eyes. *Then visit Mom and Dad on Saturday.* As for the weird water, Japan has survived worse. If Tokyo can recover from earthquakes and tsunamis, we can recover from this. It'll be over before we know it.

But by lunchtime, Haruki isn't so sure.

"Look at this!" calls Chisa Nakao from the window, peeking through the blinds. Some sunlight peeks through and catches in her hair, which is cut into a bob. "The water's risen even higher!"

Several people from Haruki's office stand to catch a glimpse of the rising water. Fear prickles along Haruki's shoulders. It must be thirty centimeters deep now.

"But where's it *coming* from?" asks their boss, Mr. Kojima. He's a serious, pinch-faced man who, at every opportunity, invites the whole office out for drinking parties. These *nomikai* are unavoidable for lower downs like Haruki, and several of the worst hangovers he has ever suffered have been because of his boss.

"The authorities don't know," says Chisa.

"Still?" Mr. Kojima shakes his head. "Well, there's nothing we can do. Back to work, please, everyone."

But the TV in the lobby has been switched to the news, and Haruki can't resist the urge to stop and watch.

"The Prime Minister has issued a mandatory shelter-in-place order until the situation can be brought under control," says a middle-aged news anchor, his face serious. "No one is permitted to leave their current location."

Haruki's eyes meet Chisa's. They widen in fear.

"We can't do that!" says another woman whose name Haruki doesn't know. "I have kids!"

Phones start buzzing and ringing, no doubt people contacting their loved ones, to ask where they are and where they're sheltering. Haruki takes his own phone out and stares at it. When it rings, it makes him jump, and he immediately thinks of Sakura. The hair salon where she works is nearby, just a few buildings away. Is she there, right now, forced to stay in her salon until the water goes away?

But it's his mother calling. Feeling foolish, he answers.

"Haruki! Are you at work?" She sounds frantic. "Did you see what they said on the news?"

"Yeah. Wait, there's flooding in Chiba, too?" Anxiety floods Haruki. He assumed the problem was in Tokyo only, but if there's water in his hometown, sixty kilometers away...

How far has this spread?

"Yes, I'll be careful. We have emergency packs here. You and Dad and Tatsu be careful, too. Does Dad still keep the emergency bottles of water in my old room? Good. All right. Bye."

None of this feels real. Is the rest of Japan having the same problem? What about the landlocked prefectures? As though in a dream, Haruki heads back to their office with Chisa. Mr. Nakamura is anxiously texting on his phone and Mr. Kojima has loosened his tie.

"Everybody take it easy for a while," he says, frowning at his computer. "I'm sure this will be all over soon."

◆　◆　◆

Andrea dearly hopes her car will be ok. She just drove forty miles in several inches of water. She thought once she reached the highway things would be okay, but it seems the flooding is everywhere. How is this possible?

"Thank you, dearie," says the middle-aged woman as she and her husband get out of the car. She barely heard the details of their California trip to visit their daughter, too stressed out about driving through so much water to listen properly.

At least up here on the hill, it's dry. Andrea can't wait to get home and take a shower. The couple's street is impressive, wrought iron fences surround massive suburban homes with manicured lawns that make Andrea want to sigh in longing. She glances at her reflection in her rear-view mirror. There are shadows beneath her brown eyes, strands of dark hair escaping from her bun.

She hastily tucks the loose hair behind her ears and fires up the engine. She and her housemate, Lindsay, live on the fourth floor, so at least the water won't affect them too much. Maybe she'll grab some things from the supermarket first so they can stock up and wait all this weirdness out.

She heads back through the suburban neighborhood and finally finds the hill leading down to the main street. Before she can reach the bottom, however, she brakes in horror. The water is even higher than before. At least two feet, far too deep for her car to pass through.

"Shit!" she whispers and reverses, panic sweeping through her. There's no way she can drive down there. She stops and gets out of her car, squinting at the streets below. People are driving towards the mountains, seeking higher ground. Others are standing on balconies and roofs, looking around in dismay. A siren shrieks in the distance. Fear floods Andrea as she claps a hand over her mouth. What the hell is happening?

◆ ◆ ◆

The cruise ship approaches the port of Nassau, Bahamas. The trip took a little under three hours and has been smooth and without incident. The crew seems happy, the passengers in good spirits and looking forward to their Caribbean vacation.

Captain Spencer frowns at the communication radio, not sure he really heard what the port just said. "Could you repeat that?"

"I'm sorry, Captain. We've restricted all inbound traffic and have ordered the immediate departure of all non-native vessels immediately. We have almost two feet of water covering the low-lying areas of the island."

"Here, too?" Captain Spencer murmurs, recalling the thin layer of flooding at Miami Port. He assumed it was a leak, something local, but the same thing is happening here, so far away. How can that be?

It sinks in what this means. "We can't come to port?"

"I'm afraid not, sir. It's underwater."

Captain Spencer sighs, rubbing the bridge of his nose. "Roger, Nassau."

The islands are a beautiful sight, the cloudless sky above them and the sun beaming down on the sparkling blue sea. And here they are, stuck, with two thousand souls who are going to be disappointed, perhaps angry, when he announces the news. He almost wants to ask Peter Swan to make the announcement, but that wouldn't do.

"We'll have to head back home," he says eventually to his crew. "We can't stay here." He prepares to make his announcement. How can he explain to the passengers that Port Nassau, maybe like Miami, is flooded? He barely understands it himself.

◆　◆　◆

"You're kidding me!"

Stephanie's father isn't the only one shouting in uproar. No one is happy about the ship having to turn around and go back to Miami. But others are staring at their phones, exclaiming to anyone who'll listen that news outlets from around the world are reporting the strange flooding.

"It's not only Nassau," Stephanie hears a young man telling the woman beside him. "It's happening everywhere. London, New York, Sydney..."

Trepidation runs through Stephanie as she glances to Callum, who is rubbing his eyes sleepily in their mother's arms, roused by the uproar.

"Maybe we should go back to our room?" she suggests. The crowds are making her anxious. "If we're going to be on the ship for a while longer."

Her mother gives an exhausted nod, and they head down the crowded stairs to their cabin. At least they have towels and beds here. Stephanie lies on hers with her Nintendo Switch, only slightly disappointed that their vacation has been cut short.

"I'm going for a smoke," her dad growls to no one in particular, and stomps off. Mom sighs when he leaves, and lies down with Callum. The cruise ship's engines roar back to life. Will things be back to normal by the time they reach Miami?

◆　◆　◆

"The lobby's flooding!"

The news travels through the building like fire. The first floor is now several centimeters underwater, the revolving glass doors halted. Moments later, their computers switch off, the lights all going out at once. Several gasps erupt and someone upstairs gives a shocked scream. They sit in silence, digesting their dark reality. Chisa starts raising all the blinds in the office and fresh light falls onto dismayed faces.

"Well, I guess we're done for the day," says Mr. Kojima, forcing a chuckle. No one else laughs. Haruki glances outside. One by one, as though in a sequence, the lights in the buildings around them flicker and die. It's already late afternoon, and it will be dark soon. The lobby is flooded, and sure enough, the roads are underwater too. Haruki stares out the window, watching a red-light blinking, slower and dimmer with every illumination, struggling to hold on. Then its battery backup dies, and it succumbs to the power outage as well.

It's surreal being in the middle of Tokyo with no artificial light. Several glows appear around him like fireflies—cell phones.

"No signal," mutters Chisa, sighing. She switches hers off.

"That's right. Save your batteries," says Mr. Kojima, like it was his idea. "No point having them on if there's no signal."

The woman from the lobby lets out a sob. "My poor children. They're in school. What's happening out there?"

They sit in silence. Haruki thinks gloomily of his apartment, of his laptop and manga comics and his clothes. They'll all be underwater now, ruined. He supposes he should be grateful he's here. Their office is on the fifth floor, safe from the flooding. For now.

He thinks of the rice ball he bought earlier and decided to save, at least until tonight. He thinks longingly of his mother's cooking. Is the flooding worse there, too? They live on a small hill, so has their house been affected? The tsunami evacuation center isn't far from their home, so maybe they're hiding out there.

Haruki grimaces. It kills him not to be able to contact anybody. It's like being cut off from the world, stuck here with Mr. Kojima and his colleagues.

The office is silent except for occasional office chair wheels rolling on the carpet. Chisa approaches him, her short hair bobbing as she drags the chair along with her. "It reminds me of 3-11," she whispers.

Haruki nods. He was twenty when the biggest earthquake in history hit the eastern coast of Japan in March 2011, killing thousands and knocking out the power for days. "It's not going to be like that," he says, seeing Chisa's scared look. "Everyone's safe." *I hope*, he silently adds.

"What if God's doing this?" she whispers.

"God?" Haruki blinks. Christianity is a religion in Japan, but he's never paid much attention to it. His parents, like most people, are Shinto Buddhists.

"You know, the Christian Bible says God flooded the earth. To punish the bad people." She gives a small, nervous laugh. "I don't really believe it, either, but if this is happening everywhere…"

"That was caused by rain, wasn't it?" Haruki glances outside. Without the city lights, the first of the stars are appearing in the dusk sky. Despite all the craziness of today, the skies have been clear and void of clouds.

"You're right." She nods. "It was silly of me to think that."

They fall into silence again, unable to do any work since the computers are off. Haruki thinks about what he brought today. His work clothes. Wallet. A bottle of milk tea, half gone, and a rice ball he's yet to eat. The thought of it makes his stomach growl, and he mutters an apology to Chisa. His thoughts turn to Sakura. If she's at work today, she'll be in her hair salon. It's near the convenience store just a block or so away. Or she'll be at home, frightened, waiting all this out. Or she'll be at her fiancé's place…

Either way, he hopes she's all right.

The mood is subdued, several people looking half-heartedly at work papers, everyone silently wondering what will happen next. Haruki doesn't have anything that might be useful in a situation like this. As though reading his mind, Mr. Kojima rises to his feet and addresses the office.

"Well, everyone, not to worry," he says briskly, like this is one of their business meetings. "The office has emergency kits in place for tsunami and earthquake emergencies. We'll start on those. They have blankets and water. We'll be completely fine until this mess is over and done with. All right?"

Several people look reassured and nod. There's the sound of several office chairs moving, and people rise to fetch the emergency kits.

"Nakao. Sato." Mr. Kojima passes them a two-person pack. "Share this one."

◆　◆　◆

"Thank you so much for letting me in," says Andrea gratefully.

"Not at all, honey! We couldn't leave you out there."

Andrea smiles in gratitude as the woman she brought home earlier, Gillian, hands her a cup of tea. The news blares on the TV, her husband Jackson relaxing in an armchair.

"Water levels continue to rise across the country," says a curly-haired news anchor. "Experts are baffled as to what may be causing it. Excessive rainfall and water main leaks have been ruled out. Some are claiming the melting ice caps are to blame. Others say it is an act of God."

The screen switches to a hillside. People are holding signs with hand-painted messages like *REPENT NOW!*, *THE END IS NIGH!*, and *THE SECOND FLOOD IS HERE!*

"Bunch of crazies," chuckles Jackson and accepts a cup of tea from his wife. He's wearing a comfortable sweater and slippers, lines around his brown eyes from a lifetime of smiling. He catches Andrea looking and gives her a wink. "Weird things are always happening, sweetie. I wouldn't worry too much."

But Andrea isn't convinced. If experts can't even find the cause of the rising water, what could it possibly be? She was hoping that watching the news would provide some answers, but she just has more questions.

"Do you think we'll be safe up here?" Gillian asks her husband, her pale hand resting on his dark one. "What if the water rises higher?"

"We're safe up here," Jackson reassures her, giving her fingers a comforting squeeze. Andrea suddenly has a memory of coming to Boulder with her ex-boyfriend, Ben. Is he okay? How about Lindsay, her roommate?

It's still mid-afternoon, and Andrea spends the day checking the water levels outside. She stays out of the way as her hosts unpack from their vacation, wondering when the water level will recede so she can finally go home. She keeps checking, hoping to find the water levels receding, but if anything, they're rising.

They're watching TV when the power cuts off and they're plunged into darkness. Without the warm light and the sound of the TV, everything is cold, still, and silent. Gillian gasps and there's the sound of rummaging. Andrea freezes in her seat, the hot cup of tea in her hands feeling strangely surreal. There's a hiss and a flash of light, and Gillian lights several candles.

"Very organized," breathes Andrea. She gets out her phone and uses it as a flashlight, helping Gillian get around until several flickering candles cast dim light around the living room. Andrea glances outside. The other houses around here are without power, too. Several people outside shout and a dog gives several frantic barks.

"I think it's better you stay here tonight, honey," says Jackson to Andrea when they've finished their tea. "We insist."

Andrea can't hide her relief. She didn't fancy sleeping in her car. "That's so kind of you. Thank you."

"We should still have a couple of slices of bread and some peanut butter." Gillian shuffles to the kitchen with a candle and starts clattering around, ignoring Andrea's weak protests. With nothing much else to do after their snack, the trio decide to go to sleep.

"I'm sure by morning everything will be better," says Jackson, his bald head gleaming in the light of the candles as they head up the stairs. "Don't you worry."

"Yeah." Andrea nods, though he can't see in the darkness. "Listen, thank you again for all this."

"Not to worry, not to worry. You can use our daughter Lauren's room. She moved out a few years ago, but we haven't changed much. It's just down here, down this hall…"

Lauren's room has a single bed and several posters Andrea can't make out in the darkness. She lies down, having no pajamas to change into, as her mind spins. She can't get the sight of the water on the road out of her head. How many people's houses are underwater now? She looks at her phone, but there's no signal. She can't even go to social media to see what's happening around the world.

Jackson's words echo in her mind. *By morning, everything will be better.*

He's probably right. America has been hit by earthquakes, tornadoes and hurricanes and things always turn out all right in the end. She turns over. Lauren's bed is really comfortable. Her eyelids grow heavy, and her thoughts float away as she drifts off.

Andrea isn't sure what woke her up, but her eyelids burn, like there was a bright flash of light. She blinks, her vision adjusting, and glances through the window.

There's a man outside. It's Jackson, she realizes. He's stumbling around the back garden like he's drunk, looking around in confusion. What's he doing out there?

Andrea grabs her purse, fighting off the debilitating anxiety that would have stopped her in her tracks a year ago. She feels her way down the stairs in absolute darkness. The front door opens as she reaches the bottom of the stairs and Jackson marches through the living room.

The candles are dying, but Andrea can see the flickering light reflected in the ankle-deep water.

"What's going on?" calls Gillian's voice from upstairs.

"It's Jackson!" Andrea calls, panic rising as the older man wades aimlessly through the water, holding his head in pain. "Are you all right, Jackson?"

Gillian's thundering footsteps join her, and she gasps. "The water's rising! We need to go. Jackson, darling, where've you been? Did you even come to bed?"

The next half hour is a blur. Gillian rushes around, drenched as she packs canned food, water, and clothes. Andrea shivers as she watches helplessly, soaking wet and clinging to her only possession, her purse. She glances outside. A dog's bark echoes through the dark, silent neighborhood. Do the other people even know the water is rising?

"We'll go to the mountains," Gillian calls. "Andrea, dear, will you help me get this to the..." Her voice trails off. In the candlelight, her blue eyes widen. "Oh, God. The car! The garage!"

As she feared, the garage is flooded, their car is submerged in water.

"Take my car," says Andrea. "I parked a little farther up the hill."

The front lawn is soaked, the grass struggling to absorb all the water. It's chilly outside as they run to where Andrea's car is parked. The water hasn't reached it yet.

Jackson stands around, looking confused as Gillian and Andrea pack the trunk with bags of clothes and blankets, boxes of food and other supplies. Andrea is impressed by how much Gillian has thought this out, and wonders if she slept at all tonight.

"Jackson, darling, get in," says Gillian after her husband has dressed. "Are you all right?"

"Yeah." Jackson blinks. The smile from last night has gone as he clambers into the backseat. "Yeah. I just feel odd. What's happening?"

"Are you going to drive, dear? It's your car."

Andrea hesitates. With no light except her headlights, she isn't sure she can drive up the mountains in the darkness.

"Because I used to go camping with my family in the mountains," adds the older woman. She has tied her curly brown hair in a bun and is eyeing Andrea's car. "I'm familiar with the roads. If you need me to drive, I will."

"Thanks," says Andrea gratefully. "I'm sorry I'm so useless."

"Don't be silly." Gillian gives her a warm smile. "Right, do you have everything? Good."

Her motherly calmness makes it feel like they're going on a weekend getaway, not escaping a catastrophe. As the headlights bathe the street in light, Andrea glances back from the backseat. The trunk is full of things, but she can still see the water creeping up the driveway, black as tar. How deep does it go now? Is all of Boulder underwater?

Tears fill her eyes as her car's engine roars to life and they crawl up the hill. Gillian tuts and sighs to herself as they make their way towards the Rocky Mountains.

"We're the lucky ones," she says.

"Yeah." Andrea glances in the direction where she thinks the town must be. All is in darkness.

❖ ❖ ❖

It's been eight hours since they were due to return to Miami Port, but the ship has been forced to stay at sea. It's dark now, and Stephanie can see lights in the city on the horizon and their reflection in the water. The flooding has gotten worse. She watches, swallowing in her suddenly dry throat. It's like the world is sinking into the ocean.

She jumps as the door slams. Dad is stomping around like an angry bull. He ran out of cigarettes a few hours ago and there isn't a soul on the ship who doesn't know about it.

"Eight hours, it's been!" he roars, throwing his hands up. "And not a single crew member to be seen! What the hell are they doing?"

The words die on Stephanie's lips. You don't interrupt Dad when he's angry unless you want a shove or worse.

"I found a guy, he said he was only a bartender. But there's something weird going on onshore."

"There is, Dad," says Stephanie, despite herself. She points at the only window. Dad comes up next to her and squints. The lights in the city are not electric, that's clear enough. They must be emergency lights, candles, fireplaces, nothing that uses electricity. Just what is going on out there?

"Well." Her dad straightens. "Fuck me."

"Don't swear, please, darling," whispers Stephanie's mom.

They're still in their cabin, reluctant to leave when so many angry people are stomping around the ship. Callum sits with his back against the wall, pouting, a half-empty bottle of water in his hand. Then the speakers crackle, and everyone sits up straight.

"Good evening, ladies and gentlemen." The speaker sounds exhausted. "Our apologies again for the delay in disembarkation, but it appears it's not possible right now to enter Miami seeing as it is several inches underwater."

They look around at each other, stricken.

"I'm sure… well, we certainly hope the authorities will have cleared it up in no time. In the meantime, we believe the safest place for you all is on this vessel. Please feel free to enjoy the casino, complimentary drinks, and other facilities in the meantime. We will keep you updated with any developments. Goodnight and stay safe."

◆ ◆ ◆

Captain Spencer is furious.

Giving the thousands of passengers free reign of the casino and the alcohol supplies might be a short-term solution, but he was never asked before the announcement. He could kill Julian King.

The captain watches as several people waver drunkenly near the poolside, partying despite the late hour. He looks through his binoculars towards the shore for the fiftieth time tonight. Is it his imagination, or is the water getting deeper? What could possibly have caused all this?

Shouting down below grabs his attention. A fight has broken out among some of the passengers. He pulls on his officer's cap and heads out, shouting to any crew members around to help break up the fight.

Two bloody noses and a black eye later, Captain Spencer orders the others to switch off the lights. "It's nearly eleven o'clock. There are children on board!" he shouts. "Barrymore, Lee, with me. King, Rhodehart, get the passengers to their cabins, please."

He mops his brow as he steps into his office with Jay Barrymore and Yvonne Lee, two of his most trusted cabin crew members. He looks helplessly at them, the shouts of the fighting drunks still echoing around the deck.

"I've never been in a situation like this before," he mutters, taking off his cap and sighing. "Do we have plenty of supplies onboard?"

"Plenty, sir." Lee's smooth voice always has a way of calming the captain. She's in her forties, her sleek hair in a neat ponytail. "We have emergency supplies and just got an order in for the boarding next Tuesday. We aren't short on food and water. For now," she adds quietly.

"Right." Captain Spencer straightens. "I want everybody reassigned to cabins in groups. Keep families and friends together, of course. Put women traveling alone or with children on the top deck. Try to find out if there are any passengers on board that are military or law enforcement and schedule a meeting with me but keep it quiet. Rotate the crew to sleep in shifts. We need to ration the supplies without creating a panic. Start a meal schedule for the passengers and eliminate the buffet. Make sure people have enough water in their cabins but ask them to minimize waste. We need to prepare for this to last longer than we might anticipate."

"How long, Captain?" asks Barrymore, his brown eyes widening. A blond man in his mid-thirties, Barrymore has worked as a cruise ship crew member for most of his adult life. Captain Spencer doesn't know why he thinks the young crew member might expect him to be able to provide answers. He changes the subject.

"You have an elderly mother at home, don't you, Jay?" he asks, his voice quiet.

Barrymore swallows and gives a nervous nod. "I'm worried about her, Captain."

"Of course you are. I'm sure the matter will be fixed in no time. However, it's prudent to prepare for the worst. Tell the others," he adds, tapping his own walkie-talkie. "It's paramount now to ensure everyone remains calm. Besides," offering the crew members a smile as he heads towards his cabin, "where better to be during a flood crisis than on a massive, well-supplied vessel? We have our very own Noah's ark here."

"Minus the animals, sir," says Lee, giving a nervous smile.

Captain Spencer glances out the window to where the fighting erupted. "I wouldn't be so sure."

◆ ◆ ◆

Captain Spencer jumps awake to the sound of clashing and banging. He leaps out of bed, bare feet slapping the floorboards, and opens the door to a wave of noise.

"What's going on?" he bellows.

The sky is cloudy, still an hour or so from dawn, gray floating across the navy sky. Crew members Swan and Robins run past him. "We got reports of some passengers breaking into the galley!"

Captain Spencer joins them, and they find several angry-looking men and a woman with boxes in their arms. Crew members are blocking the doorway to the kitchens.

"We heard you were holding back food! We need to feed our families!" says a red-faced man, a box of food in his arms. I've got two kids!"

Robins backs against the wall, terror on his face. Captain Spencer can smell the alcohol on the angry passenger's breath from here. "Now, there's plenty for everyone. We are only two days into a fourteen-day journey. We have no plans to reduce our regular food service. We are just being responsible with what we have on board. What's your name, sir?"

"Connolly," grumbles Mr. Connolly, the box shifting in his arms.

"I know you're upset, and I understand. We're all in this together," says Captain Spencer, raising placating hands. He must remain calm, for the sake of his crew. "If you put those things back right now, I promise there won't be any backlash, but we need to ensure the safety of everyone on board." He nods to the other man, whose shoulders slump. "Do we have an understanding?"

For a moment, the drunk men glare at them. After what feels like an age, Mr. Connolly finally puts down the box with a loud clatter. Relief floods Captain Spencer and he hears Lee exhale behind him. "Yeah, all right."

"Excellent. You're both free to go. Thank you for your cooperation."

"That was fantastic, sir," says Peter Swan, wringing his hands as they leave.

"See that the crew splits the supplies into the number of passengers and crew members aboard," Captain Spencer orders his crew. "And keep back twenty… eh, make that thirty percent of what we have in the backroom storage, just in case. Lee, I want a list of everyone aboard, their cabins, and the number of people in each room."

He's almost back to his cabin when it occurs to him that those last words really make him sound like the captain from *The Titanic*.

So long as this cruise ship doesn't meet the same fate.

◆　◆　◆

Stephanie lies awake that night, wondering just how much longer they're going to be here. Her mom unpacked some of the clothes for the vacation and now they're lying in the cabin, the sea is so calm it doesn't feel like they're aboard a ship at all. Dad is snoring, and after much fussing about not being allowed out, Callum finally fell asleep too. Stephanie slips out of bed, going as quietly as she can to the door. If she stays here for much longer, she'll go stir crazy.

The lights in the corridor are off, probably to conserve energy. Peace steals over Stephanie. Without her dad's grumbles and Callum's whining, it's strangely quiet. It's dark, too, but faint starlight shines through the circular windows facing the deck.

She shivers when she reaches the door leading outside, wishing she brought a cardigan. Out here, the stars are brilliantly bright, thousands of them lighting up the world. Stephanie can't see anything when she looks around, and for a moment, she wonders if they have somehow floated out to sea. But then she can see the square silhouettes against the horizon. Most of the emergency lights are off, the people of the city probably getting some sleep. It must be very late at night.

She shivers, rubbing her arms. It's nearly summer, but the deck is cold. Waves slosh gently against the side of the ship and a cool breeze washes over her, blowing her short red hair. She steps forward to look out at the water, taking hold of the taffrail. The water looks so dark from here. Behind her are dozens of unused deck chairs and up on her left is the pool area. Staring out at the dark ocean, for a moment it feels like she's the only soul left in this world.

Just as Stephanie is wondering whether there's anyone else outside tonight, shouting attracts her attention. Curious, she slips along the deck, making little noise with her socked feet. She soon finds a dozen or so people climbing into a lifeboat. It's attached to machinery that will lower it into the water.

Stephanie stays hidden, not liking the look of them. They're mostly men, though there's a woman there too, anxiety on her face and her belly swollen with pregnancy. She watches, swallowing, as they finish clambering into the boat, the pregnant woman with some help, and the boat begins to lower.

A man sticks his head out of the window and shouts something. A silhouette from an upper deck shouts something back, and they argue and bicker. Stephanie, glad for the darkness, shivers as she hides out of sight, watching from around the corner. She looks around, her breath fogging at her lips. Will anyone see what they're doing? Do they have the right idea, trying to get back to land?

A shout behind Stephanie makes her jump, and she shrinks into the shadows as a man and a woman run past, shouting.

"What do you think you're doing?"

"We're leaving!" shouts a man from the lifeboat. Stephanie can see him through the taffrail bars. The glint of a knife flashes in the starlight, perhaps stolen from the ship's kitchens. He waves it wildly at the staff trying to approach. "Don't try to stop us!"

"Those lifeboats can hold a hundred people!" shouts a blond-haired man. He's wearing pajamas but has pinned a staff member badge on the front, lopsided in his haste. "You can't take it!"

"Watch us," snarls the man. Stephanie's heart races as she watches the boat lower to the sea. Stephanie glances up, but the silhouette has disappeared.

"Stop!" The woman gives a scream as the blond man jumps onto the lifeboat. He grabs the thief and they both roll on top of the boat. Stephanie's fingernails dig into her cheeks. She is rooted to the spot, forced to watch the absurd brawl. Scared faces stare out from inside the windows as the men grunt and struggle.

"Stop it! Jay!" screams the female crew member, an Asian lady with her hair tied in a ponytail. For a moment, it looks as though the boat thief is going to sink the blade into Jay's chest, but the crew member gives a shout of triumph. With a small splash, the knife falls into the ocean below.

"You're under arrest," he pants. "All of you."

Stephanie knows what will happen, but the cry of warning has barely escaped her lips when the thief strikes Jay with a meaty fist. The crew member flops like a fish off the boat and lands with a splash into the sea.

"Jay!" screams the woman.

There's a strange silence as the lifeboat bobs on the dark water, the thief breathing hard and massaging his knuckles. Stephanie watches, her heart in her throat.

The water is still. The man isn't coming to the surface.

"Jay!" cries the woman and grabs a nearby lifebelt. She tosses it over the edge. The man on the lifeboat crouches, looking around at the water with concern. Did Jay get knocked out?

What do I do? Screams through Stephanie's mind. *Go and get help?*

The lifebelt floats innocently on the surface. In the darkness, the sea looks almost black. There's no sign of the blond-haired man anywhere.

"Jay! What's taking him so long?" the woman cries. She disappears, perhaps to the lower parts of the ship, and Stephanie watches the water, her chest constricting. She can't breathe. Surely a cruise ship member knows how to swim? But there's no sign of him, not even bubbles.

"Shit," mutters the thief, on all fours now and peering at the water. He stretches his hand towards it.

"No!" a woman shouts, her arm reaching from the boat door to grab his jacket. "Don't touch the water!"

"What are you talking about?"

"Don't you see?" The pregnant woman sticks her head out, her eyes wide as she looks at the ocean. "This lifeboat has windows underneath. Something big dragged him down into the water!"

Stephanie clenches her shirt in her fists, shivering.

"Don't you touch that water, Mark! *There's something wrong with it!*"

Stephanie has heard enough. Panting, she backs away and sneaks along the deck. She slips back inside, shivers racking her body and nausea swimming in her guts. Did that man really sink to the bottom? What did the woman mean, "something big"? Images of the lifeboat thief's knife and the man called Jay splashing into the water flash across her mind as she slides her fingers along the wall, searching for their cabin. For one horrid moment it seems she won't be able to find it, but then she spots the door to number fifteen in the darkness and slips inside, closing the door behind her.

She feels much safer when the door lock clicks closed. Rubbing her cold hands together, Stephanie finds her bed. Mom and Callum are asleep on the larger duvet, but Dad isn't anywhere to be seen, the faint starlight from the only window casting onto his side of the bed.

Stephanie listens, wondering if he's in the bathroom. She curls up into a ball beneath her blanket and closes her eyes, thrusting her hands between her knees and trying to think of something, anything, else besides Jay and the lifeboat.

◆　◆　◆

Haruki lies on the carpet under a thin blanket. Moonlight shines through the blinds of the windows and casts symmetrical stripes over the office and its occupants, some sleeping beside their desks, others stretched out in the communal area. There are no sounds that Haruki has come to associate with the city. No sirens, no rumble of train tracks, just the occasional grunt and sigh. The emergency packs provided a blanket each, several bottles of water, and instant food, but they were designed to last a few days at the most while awaiting rescue in the face of a tsunami or an earthquake. They've been here a little over a month.

Mr. Kojima insisted on closing the blinds so they won't have to see the rising water, but Haruki can't relax without knowing. He rises to his feet, letting the blanket fall to the floor with a whisper, and slips to the window. Without the lights from the city skyscrapers, the stars produce a stunning display, millions of sparkling gems illuminating the city and backlighting the staggered skyline. They capture Haruki's breath, and for a few wonderful moments, he escapes his circumstances and gets absorbed by the tranquility.

But he blinks back into reality and his eyes travel to the ground. The water is higher, perhaps three or so meters now. The whole lobby must be underwater. Perhaps even the first floor. What about the people who were working there?

No one else seems to be awake. Shivering, Haruki goes back to his space near his desk, wrapping the thin blanket around him. They are trapped here. How far does this problem go? Will help ever come? He drifts off.

He is startled awake by murmuring voices and morning light. Summer clouds have gathered in the sky, thick humidity in the air. Mr. Nakamura, their superior below only Mr. Kojima, is on his feet, saying he's going to go upstairs.

"They might have more supplies to share with us," he says, and disappears through the door.

"I don't think they will," says Chisa. Her hair is tousled, the top button of her shirt undone, a tired look on her face. "They won't have any more than we have."

As she predicts, Mr. Nakamura comes running back a few moments later, ashen faced. "They told me to get out!"

"Of course they did," snorts their boss, Mr. Kojima, like he knew it all along. "If someone from the floor below came up here asking us to share, would you say yes?"

An uncomfortable silence settles on the office. Haruki always thought people would band together to help each other during crises like these, but even the thought of sharing what few supplies they have with strangers makes him feel oddly protective. Is this a survival instinct?

"Where's Yamada?" says Mr. Kojima. Everyone looks around. Mrs. Yamada, the woman worried about her children, has disappeared from the office.

"How did she leave?" The boss stares around at everyone as though they're all keeping a secret from him. "Did she go to another floor?"

Silence reigns over the office. When was the last time Haruki saw Mrs. Yamada? He can't remember.

"I've had enough of this." Mr. Kojima gains his feet and pulls on his suit jacket. Because of the warm weather, nobody brought a coat with them. "I'm going home. I have a wife and a cat."

"Sir, isn't it best we stay here?" asks Chisa, desperation in her voice.

"You do whatever you want." The boss scowls at them. "I'm not spending one more minute here."

Several people jump as he smashes a window with his desk chair. A cool breeze washes in. The air is fresh, and Haruki blinks, the last fug of sleeping people and sweat disappearing. The office workers watch in silence as Mr. Kojima pushes his computer off his desk and picks it up, taking it to the wide office window with much grunting and grumbling. He pushes away some broken glass with the table leg and glances down at the water.

"It's black," he murmurs to himself. "Why is it black?"

Haruki and Chisa grimace at each other. He can understand their boss's desire to go home, especially if he has a wife waiting, but he can't imagine being able to float all the way home on a makeshift raft made of a desk table.

Haruki busies himself with going through what supplies they have left, trying to ignore the frustrated grunts from their boss. He finds a quiet corner and does some push-ups. A strange thought occurs to him about his local gym. Is that underwater too? He supposes it must be. A strange image of exercise equipment, weights, and mats, some floating and some firmly at the bottom of the strange black water crosses his mind as he works through his exercises. It makes him feel strangely lonely. How many businesses unfortunate to be less than three meters above sea level have been ruined by this strange flood?

The exercise makes him feel a little better, and he is on his sixteenth sit-up when the whole office gasps. Several people are by the window, peering down. It seems Mr. Kojima has managed to get the table down to the water.

"Is that supposed to be a sail?" Chisa's voice is high pitched as Haruki reaches the window, pulling on his undershirt as he goes. She glances at his bare stomach for a moment before they all glance down to where their boss is standing. The tubby fifty-something has tied his shirt to two of the table legs, oddly unfazed at being naked from the waist up. He kneels on the upturned table and bobs on the water. The lines in his face have deepened; it seems he has regretted his decision.

He glances up at the people staring down at him and wades his hands in the water, propelling himself forward. Haruki's insane desire to laugh at his boss, usually so sophisticated and domineering, clashes with primal fear. Something is wrong with the water. It's black as night, even in the morning sunshine, and with the boss's frantic paddling, it's already splashing onto the makeshift raft.

"He won't get far," someone says, and Haruki can't help but agree.

Deafening, rhythmic pulses shake the office windows and causes ripples in the water outside. Several people scream.

Some dive to the ground, others covering their ears. Terror and confusion course through Haruki. An earthquake?

A few seconds of silence and then a computerized voice booms out.

"*Do not take unnecessary risks!*" says the voice, so loud the office rattles. Chisa claps her hands over her ears, looking around in terror. Haruki's heart gallops as he crouches to the carpet while blanched faces stare at each other.

The voice rings out again. "*The water is not safe. Rations will be provided soon. Remain calm.*"

The voice fades. People pick themselves up. Haruki is sweating. The ominous voice frightened him more than anything else. Where did it come from? It sounded robotic. It reminded Haruki of Stephen Hawking's speech generator but almost nefarious, despite its reassuring message. It definitely didn't come from the building. Maybe from the *sky*?

A woman lets out a piercing scream, pointing outside. Their boss, clinging to his makeshift raft, is frozen in fear. Just ahead of him, the water is undulating from an unseen, powerful force, rapidly headed straight toward him, just below the surface. Mr. Kojima lets out a terrified cry as a dark shape bursts from the water, throwing black waves into the air. When the water settles, he is nowhere to be seen.

Several employees scream in horror as Haruki's stomach drops. "What was that?"

◆ ◆ ◆

Andrea and the Knights are not the only people who thought to flee to the mountains.

From up here, they are safely away from the rising water. Trees and lakes surround them, and if the world weren't ending, it might be peaceful here. They arrived here three days ago, driving somewhere different each day, watching frightened groups speed past them, headed to higher ground.

Andrea thinks of all the post-apocalypse movies she has seen. Their car is full of supplies. People might have guns. It's likely someone will try and take their supplies eventually if this disaster lasts much longer. If she knows anything about humans, it's that they sink to their most primal level once fear and desperation set in.

But how can she communicate this to the kindly couple who took her in? If it weren't for Gillian and Jackson Knight, she might be trapped in her apartment now, maybe on the roof and watching the water get higher and higher. How can she tell them not to help strangers who might need it when they so freely helped her?

"We're running low on gas," Gillian mutters, glancing at her husband. Jackson has barely spoken the past few days, strange considering he was cheerful and chatty the first evening they spent together. Maybe he's just worried. But at night, when they sit shivering in the car or build the tent Gillian thoughtfully packed, both Andrea and Gillian catch Jackson staring off into the distance or at the sky, a blank expression on his face.

"Are you all right, my dear?" asks Gillian one cold morning. Andrea is anxiously watching the road, a tarmac path that snakes through evergreen conifers and hills. Two cars have passed today already, children staring at her from one and the second full of rough-looking men. She wishes their supplies weren't so visible in her car. Anxiety nibbled her insides long after the men's car disappeared over the hillside.

Jackson grunts in response, staring at the horizon as though searching for something. Gillian sighs and Andrea helps her pack up the tent.

"Maybe we should sleep in the car from now on," Andrea suggests. "I'm pretty sure that was a mountain lion we heard last night."

Sleeping in the tent with two strangers is a weird experience, but at least they're all warm and dry, and with the blankets Gillian packed, it's almost cozy. They don't drive today, wanting to reserve their supply of gas, and there's a hill nearby where Andrea can look out at the town. Each time, she hopes that somehow the water will be gone, and everything will be back to normal.

Each time, she is left disappointed.

The tops of buildings can be seen among the stretch of dark water. Though the mountains surround it, there is no reflection in the black flood. It's impossible to tell from here which is Andrea's apartment building, but she has no doubt everything she owns except her car is underwater by now. It's a sobering thought. Where's her housemate, Lindsay? How about her ex-boyfriend? Is her family affected by all this? Why haven't people come to help them?

She still has her phone with her. She switches it on, but as she thought, there's no service. Sighing, she glances skyward, to where the clouds are pinked by the setting sun. There isn't a single contrail to be seen, no sign of helicopters recording a news piece on the terrible flooding. That can only mean one thing. This is happening in other places, too. Far enough where she can't get a phone signal.

In the evening, they eat a meager meal of tuna and canned peaches, Gillian insisting they save their supplies. That night, the couple sleep in the front of the car while Andrea stretches across the backseat. It's no more comfortable than the tent, but there are wild animals in the mountains.

She tries to sleep, but it's hard to relax. The couple's slow, steady breathing and the occasional hoot of an owl are all that accompanies her racing thoughts. She's impressed they can sleep at all when the whole world has gone so crazy.

She closes her eyes, willing herself to relax and sleep. It isn't until she hears the purr of an engine that her eyes open. Headlights flash across the windows, illuminating the car for a moment. Gillian stirs from the front seat.

"Someone's coming," whispers Andrea.

"Hm?" Gillian mumbles.

Something taps on the window. A man is standing outside, a basketball cap on his head and a jersey on his thick shoulders. He's chewing something, gum or tobacco, and cold horror spills through Andrea as the glint of a kitchen knife presses against the window.

"Everyone out of the car," drawls the man, and spits to the side. His teeth are yellowish-brown, and he gives Andrea a nasty grin. "Nice and slow, now."

Andrea has never been more terrified. Her body seizes in shock as she stares at the dark silhouette and his knife at the window.

"I won't ask again." His voice is cold. There's a high-pitched whine as he drags the blade down the glass, leaving a thin scratch. "Get out of the car, or I'll kill you and your parents."

Andrea opens the opposite car door, wanting to be nowhere near that man and his blade. She raises her hands, her heart galloping, her insides water. More men appear behind the first. Their jeep is parked untidily at the side of the road. There are clouds overhead, cold mountain air filling her lungs, fogging at her lips with her rapid breaths. She feels sick.

"Out, missy."

Gillian clambers out of the car and joins Andrea's side. The man is nearly at the trunk, greed in his heavy-lidded eyes, when the older woman whispers, "I knew it."

"What do you—?"

Andrea jumps a mile when a gunshot cracks through the air. She ducks out of instinct, her heart screaming, the gunshot echoing around them.

"That was a warning." Gillian stands with a pistol in her hand. The sharp scent of gunpowder stings Andrea's nostrils. The men stand stricken, the man with the knife now a foot away from the car. A small pit of ruined dirt stands a few feet away from the group. "Go on. Leave. My next shot won't miss."

Recovering, the man sneers. "You don't got enough rounds for all of us, lady."

"Oh yeah?" She holds the gun up, pointing it right at the man's chest. "You've no idea how many bullets I've got, boy. Do you really want to try your luck?"

Another gunshot. Andrea is ready for it this time, but she still jumps, her teeth chattering in her skull at the loud crack. The men all start, some jumping fully into the air.

"Fuck this," mutters one in the back. "Let's go, man. C'mon!"

"Go on, get out of here!" Gillian yells. As the men's jeep speeds off, Andrea lets out a slow breath, which turns into a frightened laugh.

"Oh my God. Good work, Gillian. Holy shit." Andrea puts a hand on her chest. Her throat is dry, and her heartbeat is pounding against her palm. She's never been so scared.

"Had to deal with our own share of racists assholes who had a problem with me and Jackson being together," says

Gillian, switching on the safety and storing the gun in her pocket. "Honey, are you all right?"

Gillian's husband is sitting in the passenger seat, his eyes wide open. Gillian grimaces. "Well, at least no one's hurt."

Andrea shivers on the back car seat. Is this how easily society can fall apart? Those men… were they always criminals, or is it desperation that led them to try to rob them?

Thank God for Gillian and her gun. Andrea wouldn't have lasted a day out here alone.

"Thank you," she whispers later and busies herself with making a hot drink for them all. The sun is rising by the time they've boiled the water and made the tea, and nobody much feels like trying to go back to sleep.

"We'll sleep in shifts tonight," says Gillian. "The one on lookout can have the gun. Have you shot one of these before?"

Andrea shakes her head. "I'm sorry."

The older woman gives her a small smile. "That's all right. You won't have to fire it. Most people get the message when you simply point it at them." She scowls. "Not all of them need *two* warning shots. Jeez."

They move off the road and find a place to stay in the trees, where Gillian parks the car between two large tree trunks. It feels safer in the small wood, hidden from people who might be spying on them from the mountains. Andrea wishes she at least had a book with her, thinking miserably of her e-reader now likely underwater back in her apartment. There isn't much to do here except organize their supplies and wait for news.

They're opening a can of soup for lunch when voices reach them in the forest. They all glance at each other and Gillian slowly takes out her gun, her mouth tightening.

"Wait," whispers Andrea. The voices aren't the men from before. It sounds like children.

"I'll go check it out," says Gillian, rising.

"No, no. I'll go." Andrea gets up. It's time she did something helpful. "Warm up the soup. I'll be back in a minute."

Andrea inhales sharp, clean air, careful not to stand on twigs as she ventures through the woods, taking care to keep the Knights and the car in sight. She's wearing one of Gillian's old sweaters, threadbare but warm, and her old sneakers. She wishes she had more than the clothes on her back. She gives a low, pained groan at the thought of all her stuff—not that she had a lot—gone. Even if things go back to normal, how will the world recover?

A child gives a delighted scream and there are pattering footsteps, like they're playing. Up ahead are several tents, two cars, and what looks like a wooden picnic table. Andrea stays behind a tree and counts nine adults, five women and four men, as well as three small children.

The gurgle of water reaches her, and she spots a small stream, big enough to step over, running clear water from a hillside. A good place to camp, with a supply of fresh water.

Look at me, Andrea thinks. She's hiding from families with kids, all out of instinct to protect their supplies. But the event from last night shook her. If it weren't for Gillian's gun, they would all be dead or worse by now.

At first glance, it could seem that the families are here on vacation. But the adults look tired, their clothes stained and threadbare, talking quietly as they look over boxes and bags.

Fear prickles up her spine and Andrea, staying hidden from sight, returns to Jackson and Gillian.

Boom.

The ground vibrates, deafening rhythmic pulses echo through the mountainside. The leaves on the trees shake with every electronic pulse. A small shriek escapes Andrea's lips. She covers her ears, panting as the children scream and run to their parents.

A voice, robotic and automated, rumbles all around her, almost too loud to bear. Did someone install giant speakers around the forest while no one was looking? Or is that strange voice coming from the *sky*?

"Cooperation is key to survival," booms the voice, the ground shuddering with every syllable. *"Ration your supplies. Work together."*

Finally, the shaking stops. Andrea lies in the dirt among the scent of soil and leaves long after the voice has departed and the whispers from the other group have cautiously returned to normal levels. Her heart is racing, tears of fright burning in her eyes. This is too much. What was that? What did the voice mean?

Finally, Andrea picks herself up and brushes dry dirt from her leggings and Gillian's sweater. Gillian rises when she sees Andrea and runs over, her face ashen.

"Did you hear that?"

"Yes! What did it mean?"

"I don't know…"

Jackson is maintaining his usual position by the fire, frowning at the car. "It was God."

"What's that, honey?" says Gillian as she runs over to stir the soup. Andrea stares at it, not so sure she's in the mood for cream of mushroom after all.

"God." Jackson looks at them both. Maybe Andrea didn't notice before, but his eyes are bloodshot. "He spoke to us."

◆　◆　◆

That night, there's a storm.

Rain falls in sudden, icy torrents, drenching them in freezing chill. They grab their stuff and bundle into the car, staring in shock at the sky.

"Is this normal for the mountains?" Andrea has to shout over the cacophony of the downpour, hail tapping the windscreen and windows so hard she fears they may break.

"Don't think so," Gillian yells back. A flash of brilliance in the sky makes them cry out in fear. Lightning.

"Let's hope it doesn't strike the car." Gillian cuddles up to Jackson, her teeth chattering. A roar of thunder crashes through the forest. The world lights up again, illuminating the frightened Knights and the car for a few seconds. Andrea buries her face in the backseat, covering her head, as the thunder lashes out at them.

Andrea has never been afraid of thunderstorms, but thoughts of tornadoes and hurricanes and the wrath of God fly through her mind as she cowers like a child. She grabs a random bag and hugs it to her chest, focusing on breathing and praying the car does not succumb to the storm.

Finally, after what feels like several lifetimes, the storm subsides.

"Is it over?" Jackson asks, his brown eyes wide as he looks outside. Andrea inhales and opens the car door. She steps out into the wood, where the air is strangely warm. Something crunches beneath her sneaker.

"Hail," she whispers, reaching down to grab it. Ice the size of her fingernail glitters in the meager light. Above, the clouds are clearing, unnaturally fast, the stars and moon coming out and shining their majesty on the forest like nothing happened. Like it was a dream.

◆　◆　◆

Andrea can't sleep that night. Every owl hoot or blow of wind makes her think of the man with the knife. She doesn't feel safe, even with Gillian and her gun. At least when the crazy storm was raging, there would be no one outside stalking their camp. When it's her turn to keep watch, she holds the cold gun in her hand. Every gust of wind or far off sound is like intruders in the shadows, and more than once she finds herself pointing the weapon into the darkness, her heart racing, sweat beading across her brow. It feels like an age before dawn finally comes.

There isn't a cloud in the sky now, the air cool and fresh like it should be. The rising water, the strange weather, that disembodied voice in the sky… could it really have been God?

Andrea is agnostic, but she grew up learning that God is a warm, loving being. That voice did not sound loving. It was cold, calculated, void of warmth. She shivers and starts rooting in a box for something for breakfast. Several weeks have gone by, yet Gillian still has a lot of supplies. That, at least, is something to be grateful for.

"Hey."

Andrea jumps a mile at the unknown voice. She whips around, a scream crawling up her throat, her heart racing as she raises the gun…

A young man is standing a distance away, his hands up. He's in his mid-twenties, with a mess of dark hair and wearing a large, bright blue parka and a startled expression.

"Whoa, whoa. There's no need for the gun."

Andrea swallows, feeling a little foolish as she lowers the weapon.

"I'm Liam," he says, taking a step forward.

"Don't come closer!" Andrea wishes she weren't shaking so much.

"I'm not going to hurt you," he says, though he doesn't take another step. "Me and my family are over on the other side of the woods. Don't you recognize me?"

Andrea blinks at him. "Uh? Sorry, no."

"That's okay." He gestures and she flinches, the gun raising half an inch again, but he rubs the back of his head, looking sheepish. "I work at the movie theater on Vine Street. I've sold you popcorn at least a few times."

"Oh." Andrea's pulse is finally slowing. "Um, right. Yeah, I think I remember you." *Why am I being so polite to this guy?* Guilt for nearly blowing his head off? "I'm Andrea."

"Right. Mind if I come a bit closer?"

Andrea makes a non-committal shrug and Liam comes over, his hands still visible. "We were wondering if you'd like to trade. We have some clothes and pillows we could trade for food if you're interested. Fresh water, too."

Gillian moves from inside the car and climbs out. "A friend of yours, Andrea?" She glances at the gun still in Andrea's hand.

"Sort of," Andrea says. "Um, this is Liam. He's with the kids on the other side of the forest and wants to trade."

Jackson suddenly gives a shout. Andrea didn't even hear him exit the car. "Don't trust him!" he croaks, pointing a finger at Liam, who looks startled. "He's the one who tried to rob us the other night!"

"Rob you?" Liam's eyes flicker between the three of them as he takes a shaky step back. "No. I wouldn't do that."

"It wasn't him," says Andrea, remembering. "That man was different. He was much older and bald."

Relief fills Liam's face. "I'm here with my parents and my little sister," he says. Andrea turns to the others.

"He says he can give us things we need," she whispers. "And they have kids with them."

"We can't suspect everyone," Gillian concurs, but she holds out her hand for the gun. "You're to keep your distance," she calls to Liam. "Nothing personal."

"Understood." Liam nods and slowly lowers his hands.

◆　◆　◆

More cars arrive in the late afternoon. Andrea and the others freeze, ready to defend themselves, but most of the cars drive right past and farther up the mountain path. Some have suitcases strapped to the roofs, curious faces looking out at them as they pass. But one blue Ford rolls up at the edge of the forest. Inside is a young couple, a woman and a man.

"Do you think we should be worried?" asks Andrea as the doors open. A woman jumps out of the passenger side and shakes out her curly hair. Andrea gasps.

"Oh my God! Lindsay!"

Andrea's roommate screams when she sees her, making Jackson jump and curse. They run to each other and embrace. Andrea inhales her familiar scent, so glad to see her she can't stop the tears pouring down her cheeks.

"I'm so glad you're okay." She holds her tight. "I didn't know where you were…"

"I looked all over for you." Lindsay sniffles. "We waited as long as we could… then we had to pack and leave. I've been worried sick, Andy! Where've you been?"

Andrea introduces Lindsay and her boyfriend, Dave, to the Knights. They relax when Andrea explains they're friends. To their delight, the young couple have brought their own tent, some packets of instant food, and blankets.

"We have a radio," says Lindsay, showing them. "It can catch a signal sometimes."

"Really?" Any news from the outside world would be fantastic right now. Lindsay puts it in the center of their camp and kneels beside it, fiddling with a dial while Andrea watches on with eager anticipation. Andrea has been taking things one day at a time here, but it isn't until she sets eyes on that little radio that she realizes how much she has missed being connected to the rest of the world. Weeks and weeks without internet or showers have driven her half-mad. Seeing Lindsay is like a breath of fresh air after months in a mine.

They drink water companionably as Lindsay messes with the radio. "It can take a while to get a signal," she says, her brow knitted in concentration. Andrea beams at her, so glad to see a friendly face. They all crouch and listen when finally, a male voice comes out of the radio. It's low and sounds beaten down, but it's definitely human. Andrea wonders if Lindsay heard that weird voice in the sky, too.

"...the United Nations has established a multinational task force to determine the origin of the water," the man's voice says and they all stare at each other. So, it is as they feared; the water has risen all over the world. How many cities lie underwater right now? How many people have drowned or lost everything?

"They are searching for a solution. Stand by. Stay safe."

"That's it for now, I think," says Dave as the voice fades and they're greeted with static. "Same message every morning and evening. What's going on out there?"

They trade some things with the family across the woods. There seems to be an unspoken agreement between the groups about territory, though Liam says they can use the stream. Andrea is relieved to see the children in the group look well cared for and fed. One little boy gives her a shy wave as she and Liam say goodbye.

"What do you think caused this?" Gillian asks when Lindsay and Dave have been with them for several days. She and Jackson and Andrea have discussed it at length, but no doubt she wants a fresh perspective.

Andrea sits next to Lindsay on the grass, their knees touching. She has never been so happy to see her friend.

"Melting glaciers?" Lindsay suggests. "Terrorism, maybe?"

Several people start talking at once. "Who could pull off a terrorist act like this?" Jackson asks. It's the most Andrea has heard him say since the night they left the Knights' house.

"And the glaciers theory doesn't make much sense, either," says Andrea. "Though it's a good suggestion," she adds when Lindsay glares at her.

"The wackos over on the other side of the forest think it's God," says Jackson in a low voice, jerking his head towards Liam's group. "They think he's punishing the world with a second flood."

"But there hasn't been any rain," Lindsay argues. "I'm sticking with my glaciers theory."

"There was rain. That weird night with the flash storm."

"But not enough to cause a flood. It's like the water came from nowhere."

"Lindsay, have you heard from Ben at all?" Andrea has held back from asking about her ex-boyfriend, but she can't anymore. "Do you know if he escaped or if he's all right?"

Lindsay's large brown eyes look at her with pity. "I don't know, Andrea. I'm sorry. When everything got crazy, me and Dave were hiding out in a park, you know the one that overlooks the city? But when the water got higher we came here. We haven't seen many other people. Just cars, but no one wants to stop. It's like everyone is afraid of each other."

"Right." Andrea looks down at her hands, remembering the last time she and Ben saw each other. They fought, like most couples who are breaking up do. She thinks of her mom, her friends, the people she's known over the years. She hasn't had time to think about people other than herself and the Knights for weeks, but Lindsay's appearance is like a gateway to the past. Is Ben okay? How about her family?

"Oh God, this sucks." Tears well up in her eyes and Lindsay hugs her tight.

"I know," she whispers. "It's okay, Andy. We're safe right now. We've got each other."

"Um, excuse me."

Liam is standing a little behind a nearby tree, wearing the same blue parka as when they first met. He's giving Andrea and Lindsay a strange look.

"Yeah, pal, can we help you?" asks Dave, rising to his feet. He's a tall man, and though he doesn't make any threats, Liam takes an involuntary step back.

"You dropped this, Andrea." Liam holds out a phone.

"Oh. Weird." Andrea's brow furrows as she takes her phone. She hasn't taken it out of her pocket since she switched it off weeks ago. "I mean, thanks."

"No problem." He looks as if he wants to thrust his hands into his pockets, then thinks the better of it. "Do you, uh, want to go for a walk?"

Andrea glances back to her friends. Lindsay gives her an *are you kidding me?* look.

"I'm not sure," she says, uncertain.

"We won't go far. I want to talk to you."

"We'll be here," smiles Gillian. "Do the kids in your camp have enough to eat, Liam?"

"What? Oh, yeah, they're fine. Thanks."

Feeling it would be ungrateful to snub him after he returned her phone, Andrea crunches through the forest brush with Liam at her side. The weather is getting warmer, summer upon them, but it's still pleasantly cool in the mountains. Who knows how freezing it will get when the colder season comes. Andrea tries not to consider the possibility that they'll still be here come winter. She glances skyward, wondering if there'll be any more strange storms.

She glances back to check the car and her group is still in view. They're talking quietly, sitting around a fire and boiling water. Lindsay thought to bring a bag of instant cocoa, something that has never tasted so wonderful to Andrea in all her life.

"What's up?" she says finally, wishing she was sitting with Lindsay and the others.

Liam's campsite is on their left, the now familiar sounds of playing children reaching her ears. It's calming, knowing that amid all this devastation, some kids are still able to have fun.

"Andrea, I was wondering if you'd like to hang out sometime." Liam looks nervous, his hands now thrust into his parka pockets.

"We're hanging out right now." She gives him a strange look. She's wearing a baggy sweater, courtesy of the trade, and her old sneakers, which get more ragged and dirtier by the day. Makeup is a distant memory, and she can't remember the last time her tangled auburn hair saw a hairbrush. It's been in a messy bun for days now. Liam couldn't possibly mean what she thinks he means.

"I've liked you forever." Andrea's eyes widen as he steps closer. "Even before all this, you know? When you used to come into the cinema, looking so cute. You were always nice to me. I'd hear you talking about the movies, and I went to watch the ones you liked, so in case I ever got to know you, we'd have something to talk about." He shifts on his feet. "Then all this craziness happened, and we're here at the same place!" He beams at her, and she takes a nervous step back. "It's like it was meant to be. A blessing from God."

"Uh…" Andrea doesn't know how to let him down gently. "Listen, Liam, you seem like a nice guy…"

His face falls, like he knows where this is going. "I *am* a nice guy. Why don't you give me a chance?"

"It's just that, now is really not the best time." She hopes she sounds gentle because she's more annoyed than anything. "You know? We don't know if it's the end of the world or what."

"All the better to grab life by the balls!" Liam takes her hand. His fingers are cold, and Andrea wants to pull away. She doesn't. "We don't know what's going to happen tomorrow, whether we'll wake up and the mountains will be flooded, too. I wouldn't have been able to forgive myself if I didn't tell you how I feel."

"Well, you have." She gently pulls her hand away from Liam's. He stands there with his own hand hovering in the air, blinking like she's slapped him. "And, um, thank you. Maybe when all this is over..." She stops talking, not wanting to commit anything. "Well, I appreciate it, but I've got to go now."

Liam takes an angry step forward and Andrea automatically throws up her arms. Gillian's gun comes to mind, and she feels stupid for not bringing it. "Don't come any closer, please, Liam."

For one horrible moment, she thinks he's going to grab her. But he swallows and nods.

"Sorry," he says. "Things have been crazy. Maybe I'm a little crazy, too." He gives a nervous laugh. "Well, see you around."

Andrea turns and walks back to her group as quickly as she dares, feeling Liam's gaze burning the back of her neck.

"What's up with you?" asks Lindsay. "Here, I made you some cocoa."

"Thanks." Andrea feels much better sitting next to her best friend, a blanket draped over her legs and a hot mug in her hand. "Um. Not much. He just wanted to talk."

It's the middle of the night when the mountain and forest once again rumbles, the deep, robotic voice echoing around the skies. They all jump awake in their tents, the faint glow of a popping, crackling fire keeping away wild animals.

"Conserve your supplies. Cooperate. Do not engage in conflict."

"Those religious nuts aren't going to let us hear the end of this," groans Dave's voice.

◆　◆　◆

"Oh, honey, thank God."

Stephanie hasn't seen her parents hug in a long time, but after days on end of not seeing her father, she isn't surprised.

Mom is holding him close, weeping into his slumped shoulder. He has a strange expression on his face, a look of confusion.

"Where have you been? Are you hurt?" Mom guides him to sit on the edge of the bed. Callum doesn't even glance up from the Nintendo Switch. Stephanie gave it to him to play with, figuring his needs were greater than hers. Their cabin still has electricity, and no one has told her not to charge it.

"And you brought supplies! Oh, darling!" A box of fresh water and instant meals lies beside the door.

"Uh, yeah. I guess I did." Dad doesn't look any worse for wear, but there's something... missing from him.

"Stephanie, sweetie, come say hi to Dad." Mom's eyes are bloodshot, relief on her face. Guilt squirms through Stephanie as she slowly approaches her father. Mom was doing her best to keep it together while Dad was gone. What went through her mind? Stephanie privately enjoyed not having him stomping around complaining about not having cigarettes. She sits beside him and gives him an awkward, one-armed hug. That's when she realizes what's missing.

His anger, the constant cloud of stress, is gone. But Dad doesn't look happy, either. He glances around at them all with confusion, like he's just woken up after being asleep for a long time.

Stephanie says nothing, though. She doesn't want to spoil Mom's happiness.

◆　◆　◆

Captain Spencer hoped the crisis would be over in a day or two, or a week at the most. It has been nearly seven weeks since their trip to the Bahamas and back, and to say things are getting out of hand would be an understatement.

Fights break out over food and water. At least ten people have been thrown overboard and haven't resurfaced. When Captain Spencer heard what happened to Jay Barrymore, he wept like a child. He loves all his crewmates like brothers and sisters, and Barrymore was one of the best.

"You're all goddamn heroes," he says to Lee. She has barely slept, in charge of getting food to the families hiding away in their cabins. "All of you."

"We'll get through this, Captain." She gives him a chaste hug, earning a small chuckle from him.

"How are we doing for supplies?" He half-jogs alongside Lee as they head down to the cabins. A small group of men lean against a nearby taffrail, giving them challenging looks and leering at Lee.

They head inside and down some steps. The captain takes out a set of jangling keys and they let themselves into the private lower deck where they keep the emergency supplies. Captain Spencer is reluctant to dig into them, but they have to take inventory and plan for a possible future.

They both pause halfway down the dark stairwell. There's a noise at the bottom, like rummaging. Rats, maybe?

But they find crewmate Robins at the bottom, rooting through some of the instant meals.

"What are you doing?"

Robins jumps a mile, turning with a scared look in his eyes. Everything about the way he's crouching and the fright on his face is wrong to Captain Spencer.

"I wasn't doing anything," Robins babbles. But the pile of boxes against the wall say otherwise.

"You were in here earlier." Lee steps forward. "I let it slide, but… are you hoarding supplies?"

"N-no!"

"Show me," says Captain Spencer, his voice calm. Trembling, Robins glances over at a sheet half covering food he's been hiding.

"Disgusting," Lee says. "There are kids on board and you're keeping all this stuff to yourself! I suppose it was you who let the lifeboat down?"

Robins swallows and gives a frantic nod.

"Jay died that night!" Lee bellows. With remarkable strength, she drags him up the stairs.

"Lee!" The captain shouts after her, but she doesn't listen. They burst into daylight, onto the lower deck, Lee still dragging Robins by the scruff of the neck. "Lee, wait!"

"You're a dirty thief, Robins," Lee snarls in the frightened man's face.

"Who's a thief?"

Several men approach the commotion and turn their attention to Robins. "He's that arrogant prick who told us there was no more alcohol," says one, pointing at Robins. Lee falters, looking at them.

"Let's everybody calm down," says Captain Spencer. "Lee, let him go, please."

Lee's jaw tightens as she throws Robins away from her. He coughs and rubs his throat.

"We heard you say thief," says another man, looking at Robins with interest. "Someone been hoarding food, huh?"

"We're starving here, and your crew members are taking everything for themselves?" asks another man, a wild look in his eyes.

"That's not what's happening at all!" says the captain. "My crew members are doing their best to get enough food to everybody."

"I've had enough of you, old man!" the guy snarls. Captain Spencer steps back. He may be the captain of the ship, but what authority does that hold, surrounded by angry, hungry people?

"Let's go," Lee mutters, and he doesn't need telling twice. They turn and hurry up the deck and don't look back until they're at the top of the steps.

A scream makes them turn around.

"Robins!" gasps Lee, leaning over the taffrail. The men surround Robins, who's cowering on his knees.

An enormous man grabs Robins and hauls him to his feet. "I knew the crew couldn't be trusted! They're all in this for themselves!"

"Throw him over!" a woman shouts, and they yell and cheer in agreement.

"Don't." Captain Spencer grabs Lee's arm as she makes to run down the steps. "You'll get hurt, too."

The men roar and shout as they grab the screaming Robins to the edge of the deck, closer and closer, and throw him over. He yells during his descent and splashes into the water below.

"They've turned into animals," Captain Spencer whispers, his stomach plummeting. Robins does not resurface.

A sound suddenly roars across the entire cruise ship. Several people clamp their hands over their ears and look around. Captain Spencer grabs the rail as Lee holds his shoulder. The sound is so powerful the cruise ship rocks by the disturbed water. Pulses vibrate through the air like shockwaves, so loud he feels his head might burst.

"Prepare for rations," says a robotic voice. Too loud for a ship announcement. It echoes all around, like it's coming from the sky. Captain Spencer looks up at the clouds, as though he'll see the source. *"Prepare for rations."*

"Rations?" gasps Lee. "Does that mean…?"

Cheers ring out from the group of passengers down on the deck. Dark shapes emerge from the clouds. Enormous pallets carrying boxes and boxes, tied to large, powerful drones.

"It's the government!" Lee gasps as people swarm to the edge of the deck. "Are they rescuing us?"

Captain Spencer has been too stressed to feel any emotion beyond despair these past weeks, but his stomach groans in longing as the first of the drones drop off the pallets. Men and women jump upon them like starving animals, ripping open boxes and holding bags and bottles of food and water in the air like prizes.

"Get the security team down there," says Captain Spencer into his walkie-talkie. "Deck A. Rations have arrived!"

◆ ◆ ◆

"Prepare for rations."

Stephanie jumps upright at the automatic voice roaring outside, her heart pounding. Dad and Mom are awake, too. Mom's green eyes are wide with fresh fear.

"What is that?"

"Prepare for rations."

Is it another boat, coming to save them? Stephanie peeks out of the round cabin window, but there's nothing to see except the port of Miami, still underwater. Only the tops of tall buildings are visible now.

Mom looks at Dad, like she always does. He just closes his eyes again, his chest rising and falling. He's been eerily calm after he came back, and whenever they've asked him questions about where he was, he said he was "walking around the ship."

"I'll see what's happening," says Stephanie, climbing out of bed. She's sick of this room.

"Mommy, I'm hungry," whines Callum.

"I know, darling. Shh."

Stephanie has almost reached the door when there are several frantic knocks. "I've got food!" calls a voice.

"Open it, Steph!" gasps Mom. Stephanie wrenches the door open and comes face to face with the crewmate who was there on the deck the night Jay fell in the water.

"Here." The lady thrusts a heavy cardboard box into Stephanie's arms. "Are all of you accounted for? Your family's all here?"

Stephanie nods.

"Stay in your cabin." The woman is breathless, several more heavy boxes behind her on a service cart. "It's not safe out here. There's enough in there for a week."

"Thank you," says Stephanie, but the woman is already gone, knocking frantically at the next door.

Grimacing, Stephanie brings the food into the room, the heavy door closing behind her. Mom gives a moan of pleasure and rips open the box.

"Breakfast," she beams. Stephanie knows Mom hasn't eaten in at least two days, insisting on giving everything to Callum and Stephanie.

"We need to stay in here, I think." Stephanie's eyes travel to the cabin ceiling. From here, they can't hear much except the occasional thud or shout. "At least for now."

That night, the cruise ship roils as a vicious storm attacks the sea. Stephanie has never feared thunder and lightning, but there's something deeply unnerving about the flashing lights and cracking thunder rumbling across the sky. The sea churns beneath them, and anxiety twists her belly as the ship rocks and sways.

Callum cuddles up onto Stephanie's knee, his thumb in his mouth, watching the storm with tired eyes.

"You're not scared, huh?" she murmurs. He shakes his head. "Brave boy." She kisses his brow, something she rarely does, and holds onto his innocent warmth as the storm rages on.

◆ ◆ ◆

Haruki sits under his desk, Chisa shivering beside him. They've been stuck in this office for so long now. The monotone voice that accompanied the drone deliveries warned them to conserve their supplies but they're running low. And to make things worse, another violent thunderstorm forms in seconds.

Several people scream as a series of lightning bolts illuminate the office. They've used parts of broken tables to cover the window Mr. Kojima smashed, but even with the blinds drawn, the roaring wind and vicious thunder rocks the building like an earthquake.

"It'll be over soon," he shouts to Chisa. Though she's right beside him, the crashing of the water outside and cacophony of the storm makes him have to yell.

Then it's over, like God has flicked a switch. Panting, Chisa slowly crawls from beneath the desk and peers outside. Haruki's analog watch is still working, marking it mid-afternoon. The storm has left thick humidity in the air, but Haruki is becoming used to being coated in sweat most of the time.

"It's over," Chisa confirms, and people crawl out from their hiding places. Some have used files or briefcases to cover their heads.

Another window has broken in the weird flash storm, shattered glass glittering on the carpet in the corner. They all watch as the black water sloshes, restless, like the stomach of an enormous beast. The clouds, gray and thick, sit above them.

Chisa fans her damp face. "I hate summer. What I wouldn't give for the air conditioner to work." She casts a woeful look at the useless cooler above their heads.

There's a bang at the office door and everyone whips around. "It's us, from the floor below!" shouts a woman's voice. "Please, let us in! Our floor is flooding!"

Everyone glances at each other. "Don't let them in," says Mr. Nakamura. He's lost weight in the recent weeks, his belt flapping as he walks. His round belly has receded after weeks of no beer or ramen noodles. "Remember when I went upstairs, and they kicked me out? No, we need to keep to our own floors."

"Hello?" The banging continues.

"What happens when the water gets deeper, and we have to move up?" says Chisa. It looks as though she might wilt beneath Mr. Nakamura's glare, but she stands up straight and folds her arms. Admiration ripples through Haruki. It seems the disturbance of usual office hierarchy has leveled the balance of power. He can't imagine Chisa having talked back to Mr. Nakamura before this all happened.

Mr. Nakamura grunts and turns away.

"Come on." Chisa gestures to Haruki. They both reach the door and open it. A woman is standing there, two more behind her, and two men. All of them are carrying emergency backpacks and bags. They share the same haunted, exhausted look as those in Haruki's office.

"Thank you," says the woman who knocked, her graying hair in a snarled bun, her office wear worn and stained. "The water started coming under the door... we didn't know what else to do... do you have any food?"

"No more than you do," says Haruki before he can stop himself. The drones with the supplies came weeks ago and there has been no sign of the strange, disembodied voice.

"Is this all of you?" Chisa asks in surprise as the five office workers step nervously into their office. Haruki and Chisa's co-workers, twelve of them in total now that Mrs. Yamada has gone, stand or sit and watch them in silence. There is no bowing, no quiet murmur of, "good work" or "let's cooperate." The last few weeks stuck here with meager supplies, no showers, and no electricity have stripped them of the usual social airs.

"There's some room over there." Haruki gestures vaguely to some empty desks and chairs, void of computers. His thoughts float to the hole in his office chair where he's stuffed his spare rations. He feels like a small animal storing food for winter.

Fanning his sweating face, Haruki wishes it *was* winter. He'd rather be wrapping himself in blankets in freezing December than surviving in this sweltering humidity. They can't escape it.

"What's the date?" someone asks.

Mr. Nakamura has a calendar on his wall, half of the days in July marked off with big red Xs. "Fifteenth."

"Two months since this hell began," sighs a young man with glasses. "I've only been here at this office since March."

They settle by the spare desks, an unspoken agreement going through the office that the workers of the floor below are to stay on the other side. Haruki does some push-ups, determined to continue with his exercises. Something tells him it's more important than ever to be in shape now.

They divide the remaining food into fourteen and keep to their own cubicles. Strange how this was just a workspace before this whole mess, now it's almost like a home. A nest.

The thought brings a bitter smirk to Haruki. They've been reduced to animals, hoarding their food and building crappy makeshift beds.

"Did you hear that?" asks Chisa.

Haruki glances at her. "Hear what?"

He hears the second one. It sounds like a splash. Several people rush to the windows and glance out. A man and a woman are in the water, swimming through the black, their shouts lost. Someone screams as a third shape falls past the window and into the water with a huge splash.

"What's going on?" says Mr. Nakamura. "Are they trying to swim?"

"Did they jump?" asks someone.

A shape glides through the water, something massive, with deep black skin. Chisa grabs Haruki's bicep, her fingernails digging into him as the approaches the nearest man.

"Look out!" Mr. Nakamura waves at them, trying to get their attention. "Oy! Watch out!"

They don't stand a chance. The doggy-paddling man screams as the shape lunges at him from below the surface. It drags him under before he can even scream.

"Come back!" Haruki screams at the others as they splash in the water, shouting and sobbing. "Get back in here!"

The woman tries to swim for the office building, but she isn't quick enough. Chisa buries her face in her hands, her sobs lost to the screams as the creature drags them to their deaths.

◆ ◆ ◆

Each day, they hope the strange presence in the sky will speak to them, that more precious supplies will be lowered to the windows. But the skies stay silent. One day, Chisa is fiddling with the emergency radio when a voice finally comes through.

Everyone jumps and huddles around. It's been weeks since any of them heard a voice that isn't one of their own. A man is talking is on the air, static almost overpowering his low murmur, which is strangely monotone like he's reading aloud.

"Most people have fled the cities and found refuge in the mountains. The Imperial Family are currently staying in the Japanese Alps."

"Who cares about the Royal Family?" Mr. Nakamura snarls. Several people shush him.

"Death reports continue to come in. Most of Tokyo is gone, Yokohama is underwater, and many towns and cities by the coastlines have been lost to communication for weeks. Authorities are working with the American government to find a way to move forward. Stand by."

Frustration washes over Haruki as he collapses beside his desk chair. Hopelessness fills him.

"You know, I would really hate to die at work," Chisa remarks later. Despite himself, Haruki gives a snort of laughter at the dark joke. He looks outside to the next building. He's been looking at it for several days now, at the convenience store on the eighth floor. Thoughts of instant noodles, rice balls, and beer fill his mind and his empty stomach gives a low rumble.

"There'll be food there," he whispers to her as they settle to sleep that evening. There isn't much to do besides talk and eat and work out, and even Haruki is taking it easy on his exercises as it makes him hungry and thirsty.

"There'll be people there too," whispers Chisa. "And they won't appreciate you showing up to take the food." She looks at him warmly, as if she is really noticing him for the first time. "You look good with a beard."

Haruki smiles, running a hand over his hair-covered chin. Without being able to shave, his facial hair is longer than it has ever been. "Pity beards aren't allowed in the office."

The next morning, Haruki jumps awake to see Mr. Nakamura standing above him. He discarded his tie weeks ago, and there's dark stubble on his chin and yellowish stains around the neck of his shirt. With his too-wide eyes, he looks close to insane.

"You have food."

People stir at his comment, turning to stare as Haruki rises to his feet.

"What?"

"I saw you. You have food in your chair." Up close, Mr. Nakamura stinks of sweat. Perspiration dots his stubbled upper lip. The thick humidity makes it hard for Haruki to think straight, but his heart begins to race at his senior's words.

"Just been rationing." Haruki shrugs like it's no big deal even as his instincts call to him to shove Nakamura away from his space. "I got the same as everyone else."

"Look, I'm starving here. You should share. You're the youngest." He grabs the front of Haruki's shirt. Haruki pushes him and the older man stumbles back.

"You little—"

"Mr. Nakamura, we have a plan!" says Chisa desperately. Nakamura glances at her. "There's a convenience store on the other side of the water over there."

"If it's across the water, it might as well be in Australia," growls their senior, but he doesn't try to grab Haruki again.

"Then we'll build a raft!"

Haruki forces himself not to groan. It didn't go well for the last person who tried to build a makeshift boat out of here.

Nakamura grunts and leans against the opposite desk. "I'm sorry, Sato," he says to Haruki. "I'm just… I'm so worried about my family."

"We're all worried about our families, sir." Haruki has to force himself to say the last part, but they can't fall apart now. As soon as two people start fighting, that'll be the end of the fragile sanctuary they have built here. "And we're all hungry. Look." He pulls out a small protein bar from the hole in his chair, the baser instinct in him snarling at him not to share. He presses it into Nakamura's pudgy fingers. "You can have this, but don't ask me again."

It feels strange to be talking to his superior like this, but times are strange. Politeness and manners don't help you survive.

Nakamura gives a small nod and shuffles back to his space. Haruki stands straight, silently daring others to ask him. Nobody does.

That day is spent testing the strength of the largest table in the office. The biggest desk is used to holding several computers. They flip it and test it, balancing it on two other desks and standing on it for balance. Haruki tries to imagine the sea moving below him on this makeshift raft, and more than once, he wants to chicken out.

But there's no guarantee that strange voice in the sky will send more supplies, and if they wait much longer, they'll be too weak from malnutrition to attempt anything. They can't venture to the upper floors without more supplies when the water gets higher. What if they're turned away?

"That won't work," says Chisa as Haruki jumps back to the ground. "You'll sink."

For a moment, annoyance threads through him at her pooh-poohing his idea, but she sees the fear in her eyes. She's worried he'll drown just like Mr. Kojima did.

He forces his voice to stay light and even. "Do you have a better idea?"

Chisa holds up a plastic bottle, one of the many empty ones they have from the emergency packs. "It's worth a try."

They tie together dozens of empty bottles with string from the stationery drawer, the survivors only too glad to give up their waste. Those who aren't helping watch with interest as Haruki, Chisa, Nakamura, and several others help build a wide raft, finally breaking apart a spare office chair and attaching the seat to the top.

"This is… precarious," says Haruki, examining their handiwork. "Are you sure it'll work?"

"No," says Chisa. She looks terrified now, a light sheen of sweat on her forehead. "Maybe this isn't a good idea."

"I'd rather drown than starve to death," says Haruki firmly. He looks around at all the survivors. Many have pitched in with helping with the string, accepting that Haruki really is going to try and make the trip to the next building. Mr. Nakamura sits against his desk, arms folded, watching with something that looks strangely like jealousy.

"Right. Listen up, everyone." Haruki is a confident man, but fifteen pairs of eyes turning to him at once make him almost falter. "We're going to tie some rope from the emergency packs to this raft. Everyone's going to help pull me back in when I'm ready to return."

"And how are you going to get there?" asks a voice. It's a guy from downstairs; Haruki doesn't know his name.

"I'm going to row." He holds up a chair leg. It's not ideal for an oar, but it's the best they've got. He picks up his now empty emergency rucksack. "Anyone want anything?" he jokes. When no one responds, he grabs one of the radios, a blanket, and several papers.

"What are you doing?" Mr. Nakamura asks.

"Taking things to trade," Haruki explains. "There might be people there. They won't respond well to me showing up and asking for free stuff. But they might be happy to have a radio."

He snatches up some pens at random and stuffs them into the bag.

They decide to try and go in the early morning before it gets too hot. There hasn't been any crazy weather for three days now, and when the sun rises the next morning, a cool breeze on the air, Haruki's hopes are fairly high.

The water is higher than it was when Mr. Kojima made his failed escape. Haruki tries not to think of their boss's demise. Their raft is stronger, he is much fitter than the middle-aged boss was, and they have a realistic purpose of where they're going.

The rope is firmly tied to the raft, and Haruki gives a few experimental pulls. It seems strong enough. They lower the raft to the water below. There isn't much space at all now between the broken window and the surface of the black water. The sky is mostly clear, and Haruki hopes they won't have a freak flash thunderstorm.

But it's too late to back out now. These people are relying on him.

"Be careful," says Chisa, anxious as Haruki lowers himself from the window, glad he has kept up with his exercises. His feet touch the raft two meters below. It wavers on the water and he hisses through clenched teeth, trying to find his balance. Chisa gasps as he finally finds purchase. Breathing slow, he lowers himself onto the raft.

It's uncomfortable, hunched on the office chair seat, trying not to move and compromise his balance, his legs tucked in front of him. The building with the convenience store suddenly seems much farther away than before.

"Are you all right?" Chisa calls. She and a few others are staring out of the window, the rope in their hands.

"Yeah," Haruki calls back. "Okay, I'm going to start rowing. Let the ropes go slack as I go. If we run out of rope before we get there, we'll have to figure out something else. When I get there, I'll take one of the ropes. Pull me back with the other one."

His heart is racing, but he gives them a confident smile.

The water is black like tar, splashing against the plastic bottles. The raft, which seemed so innovative yesterday, now seems laughably juvenile. But Haruki can't back out now.

Trying to find confidence in the fact his fellow survivors have the rope and can pull him back if there's danger, Haruki dips the chair leg into the water. The boat bobs and sways, making him suck in a terrified breath. Will it even go?

But with several more deep, slow strokes, the little raft moves forward in the water. Even though it's early morning and the sun has barely started to rise, summer's heat already settles on Haruki, thick and warm. He breathes hard, listening to the splashing, the buildings peeking at him from the corners of his eyes. The building with the convenience store isn't *that* far. Things are going well. He might even make it.

The rope slowly slacks along with his progress. He imagines them all watching him, his ridiculous little boat, wondering if they'll see him alive again.

Well, if I make it back with food and water, I'll be hailed a hero, Haruki tells himself, his tongue between his teeth as he rows again. Slow and steady does it.

Haruki's throat is already horribly parched, his stomach empty. His arms already hurt from rowing, his lack of food making him weak. He badly wants to rest, but the only thing that sounds worse than continuing is stopping.

When he's three-quarters of the way there, a movement in the water catches his eye.

He almost drops the oar in his fright. Something moved beneath the water. He was so worried about building a competent raft he nearly forgot about the mysterious creatures that took Mr. Kojima and the others.

He swears beneath his breath, paddling harder. The rope goes taut and slackens as he goes. His pulse races, his breathing quick as he frantically paddles, feeling like a panicked fish. The shape moves right beneath the surface, and Haruki catches sight of something large and scaly.

He has almost reached the building. Though the lights are off, Haruki can see the familiar strip of blue marking the convenience store, and his heart lifts. The oar splashes in the black water as he breathes hard and fast, hating how vulnerable he is, hating how he talked himself into this mess...

He gives a small cry as the boat suddenly lurches. Whatever's underneath the water is trying to tip him out.

"No!" he growls as he hits the side of the building, feet pressing against the edge of it. He can *feel* the thing beneath the water, circling him like a bird of prey. Nausea bubbles in Haruki's stomach. He has to stand to reach the balcony above.

The raft lurches again, and Haruki imagines jagged teeth attacking the plastic bottles. Praying they will hold, Haruki grabs one of the ropes leading back to the office. He yanks it three times, and it goes slack. Panting hard, Haruki pulls it as fast as he can, watching it move like a snake in the dark water, then ties it around his waist.

He leans against the wall and slowly pulls himself to his shaking feet. He throws the oar up then grabs onto the ledge.

"Come on, Haru," he growls to himself and pulls, his arm muscles screaming as he yanks himself up. The raft sways and lurches beneath his toes as, gasping through clenched teeth, he gets onto the balcony and onto wonderful solid floor.

An exhausted giggle bursts out of him as he lies there, inhaling the scent of concrete and old tobacco. Right before him is the convenience store.

The rope around his waist suddenly grows taut, yanking him towards the balcony. Pain erupts around his torso as the rope grows tight, threatening to snap. Terror floods him as he grabs the rope and looks down. Something huge is attacking the raft.

"Hey!" Haruki bellows, grabbing the rope and pulling it. The raft comes up, black water dripping from it and onto the surface below. The other rope, the one still attached to his office, grows slack as Haruki hauls the raft onto the safety of the balcony. He checks it for damage, wiping the sweat from his brow. Two of the bottles are broken with jagged teeth marks.

What the hell was that? A shark? Haruki peers down into the water, wondering if he will ever have the courage to venture back in. There is no sign of the creature that stalked him.

Haruki goes to the glass doors of the convenience store and peers inside. A dark shape suddenly appears in the doorway.

"Who's there?"

"Has someone come to help us?"

"I'm here to trade," says Haruki. After the showdown with the sea monster, he feels oddly fearless. "I'd like to swap some things I brought for food."

There's a pause, then grunting and the sound of the glass door, usually automatic, being shoved open. A man around Haruki's age stands there, wearing a builder's baggy pants and a towel around his head.

"Show me your hands."

Haruki raises his palms. "No weapons here, and I came alone."

"How?"

Haruki gestures to the raft. "I'm from the office over there. I'm Haruki Sato. Can I come in?"

The man backs into the convenience store. "Murata."

A woman and a little girl are sitting on a blanket by the counter, the mother glancing up with fearful eyes as the girl, maybe around five or six, is playing with what must be the man's hard hat. There is a scattering of small toys around her. A convenience store employee – Haruki can tell by his uniform – sits with her arms around her legs, her eyes out of focus.

"Do you have any food?" Haruki asks, seeing no reason not to cut to the chase. Making slow movements, he lowers his bag to the ground. "I'd like to trade for some of these. Pens and paper, a radio…" He pulls out everything he brought. Murata eyes the radio.

"Yeah, there's some stuff in the back."

Predictably, the shelves of perishables—rice balls, cakes, and sandwiches, are all empty. These people must have eaten well for the first couple of weeks, at least. In the back, Haruki grabs protein bars, instant noodles, packet curry, microwavable packets of rice, potato chips, and bottles of water. He gets some gas canisters for the portable gas cooker and shoves them in the backpack. Then he grabs one bottle of a sports drink, and takes several heavenly gulps, downing most of the bottle in one. He sighs in bliss, leaning his forehead against the cool wall.

His gaze falls on several boxes of alcohol.

He grabs fourteen beers, one for each member of the office, a small smile on his face. When the bag is bulging and he has filled every pocket with food and water, he heads back into the main part of the shop.

"Help yourself," he says to the little girl, who's looking at the pens and paper he brought. She drags them over to her and begins to draw.

"Thank you," whispers the mother. "And thank you for the radio. We've been cut off from the outside world for so long…"

Murata is already fiddling with it, a frown on his face as he turns the dial with gentle precision, searching for a signal.

"I have to be getting back." For one selfish moment, Haruki considers staying in the convenience store with these people. He isn't looking forward to the journey back, and there's way more to eat here than at the office. But he squashes that desire immediately. He can't leave his fellow office workers to wait for him forever. "Listen…" He hesitates, wondering what words of support he can offer these people. "Things are going to be okay, I promise."

The mother gives him a tired smile and Murata nods to him as Haruki pushes open the store's sliding door, breathing in the thick, hot air. His raft awaits, the rope stretched between the balcony and the office window. Several people wave at him and he waves back, the backpack now heavy on his shoulders but reassuringly full of food and drinks. He feels better already.

"Right, here we go," he mutters, looking out at the dark water. Whatever beast stalked him earlier seems to have gone. Imagining enjoying a well-deserved beer once he makes it back, Haruki lowers the plastic bottle raft back into the water. He watches it bob on the surface for a few moments, waiting for a fin or a tooth, but all is quiet.

He glances over along the building's balcony. From here, he can just about see the area where his ex-girlfriend Sakura works, the hair salon. Was she at work when all this began? How do you survive surrounded by nothing but hair products?

He can't think about her now. Wherever she is, he hopes she's safe, but everyone is in the same position. His thoughts move to his family, along with a squirm of guilt that Sakura came to mind before they did. Now with his backpack reassuringly full, the immediate threat of starving or dying of dehydration has been pushed aside. Is his family still in their home, safe on their hilltop, or has the black water reached them by now? How about earthquake and tsunami shelters? They're designed with rising water levels in mind, so surely they're safe.

Hopefully he'll last long enough to find out.

The journey back is terrifying, but there's no sign of the strange scaly creature that attacked his boat. Letting the steady pull of the rope drag him to shore, Haruki glances at the cloudy sky, afraid he'll soon see a flash of lightning or falling, otherworldly rain or hail.

"Haruki! You made it!" Chisa gasps as his raft floats to nudge the side of the office building.

"Don't sound so surprised," he says, forcing his voice to be light. He won't feel safe until he's back inside that office.

Chisa suddenly screams and Haruki throws a look behind him. Something enormous is moving towards them, cutting through the water.

"Get me up!" he yells, rising to his feet and jumping, cold fear flooding him. Haruki grabs the rope, and they tug. Something snarls below him, the water churning and frothing as the plastic bottles pop and break.

Haruki curses. He didn't come this far just to be eaten by some horrible sea monster.

"Move it!" yells the bespectacled man from downstairs, his face purple as he pulls the rope. Haruki howls in pain as they pull him over the window ledge, a bit of broken glass on the frame digging into his side.

He collapses on the ground as the monster below attacks his raft. The rope suddenly pulls tight, and people gasp.

"Let it go! Leave it!" Haruki growls.

The rope slides from their hands and whips the water below. They all stare out of the window while Haruki lies panting on the carpet. He reaches his hand to touch his stinging side, and it comes back red.

"Are you okay?" Chisa kneels beside him, blinking in horror at the cut.

"I think so." He pulls up his shirt. The cut isn't deep, just long. "Bit of glass got me."

Chisa runs for the first aid kit. "At least we've got this," she says and busies herself with cleaning his wound. Haruki isn't badly hurt, but he lets her work, watching as the office staff back away from the window, grimacing at each other and shaking their heads.

"That raft's gone," says Mr. Nakamura, looking around the office with a blanched face. The noise has ceased. When Chisa has dressed his wound, Haruki looks below. All that's left of the raft is a couple of broken plastic bottles and bits of string.

"You saved me," he says, looking around at everyone. His skin crawls at the thought of how close he had come to meeting Mr. Kojima's fate.

"Did you save *us?*" says one of the women from the floor below, crossing her arms. Wincing as the cut in his side flares, Haruki takes off his backpack.

"Food," moans Chisa in delight as they unpack it, pulling out bags and bottles.

"And beer," says Mr. Nakamura. "It's been so long since I had alcohol."

It doesn't have quite the effect Haruki imagined, everyone sipping warm beer in silence and muttering about why he wasted backpack space on alcohol. A hot flush creeps across Haruki's cheeks and he marches away from them, pacing around what used to be Mr. Kojima's private office. Let *them* risk their necks to get food if they are so much better at it.

He glances at the office safe. No one has bothered trying to pry it open. What would be the point? There is irony in the fact that cash is useless now. They would be better off burning it when the weather grows colder.

It's a sobering thought, that they might still be here when winter rolls around. Just how much longer is this nightmare going to continue? What will they do when they run out of food completely?

"Mr. Sato?"

"Just call me Haruki," Haruki sighs. "I think we've been through enough to be able to drop the pleasantries, don't you?"

"Right," says Chisa nervously from the doorway. "I know it must be frustrating. It's just… people are scared, you know?"

"I don't know what they expected." Haruki tries to remain calm, but the cut on his side, the close encounter with the sea monster, and people's indifferent attitude has rubbed him the wrong way. "For me to grab crates of their favorite foods and haul it back on a rope?"

"They're grateful. I am, too," says Chisa softly. She does something she's never done before and takes his hand. Haruki swallows. It's been ages since he felt any kind of physical affection, and something flips in his belly. "You were amazing. You must have been so scared."

"Yeah, well," he says gruffly, not pulling his hand away. Her fingers are warm, and something about her touch calms him. "Well, at least we're sorted for a couple of days."

When they walk back into the office, some people are arguing.

"You said there was one beer for everyone!" says a woman, pointing an accusatory finger at Haruki.

"There is," he snaps back, getting tired of their ungrateful attitude. "Fourteen beers."

"There's one missing," someone complains. "I didn't get one."

Haruki looks around at everyone, counting the cans. He drank his already, and Chisa is holding hers. Mr. Nakamura is sitting on his desk with his in hand. Haruki's eyes travel over everyone, at the desks and chairs, when…

"Mrs. Yamada?"

Everyone turns to look at a thin woman with bedraggled hair, clutching a can of beer to her chest. "It's been so long since I had beer," she says. "Thank you for fetching it, Mr. Sato."

Haruki steps forward, confusion filling him. Mrs. Yamada went missing weeks ago. Everyone assumed she jumped from the building and tried to get home to her children. But now she's blinking among them, looking nervously around as they stare back.

"Where did she come from?" Mr. Nakamura crumples his can. "Yamada? Where have you been?"

"What do you mean?" Mrs. Yamada's shoulders are tense, like she's bracing for someone to rush at her. She is totally different to the outspoken lady who made herself heard when the disaster first struck. But it's undoubtedly her.

"Nakamura, leave her alone," says Haruki. No matter where she's been, Mrs. Yamada looks exhausted and ill.

"What about my beer?" demands the man.

"Are you really going to kick up a fuss about beer?" Chisa snaps, to general shock. "Haruki got us all food and gas canisters. We should be grateful. C'mon, let's make some dinner."

When everyone curls up to sleep that night, bellies full of instant curry and rice, he is glum. He had hoped his arrival with food and drinks would bring everyone together, but suspicion and disappointment fill the air.

"Why do I bother?" he whispers to himself and closes his eyes.

He's awoken by a shrill scream.

Haruki bolts awake, smacking his head on the underside of his desk. Groaning, black spots bursting across his vision, he crawls out of bed and looks around.

"What's going—"

Several more people jump awake, the ones closest to the door clambering onto desks with their backpacks in their arms. Black liquid is seeping across the floor, coming from the crack beneath the office door. A potted plant, dead and shriveled after weeks with no care, falls on its side.

"The water!" shouts Mr. Nakamura from on top of his desk. "It's here!"

"What do we do?" a woman cries.

Haruki snatches up his bag and blanket, his heart hammering. They can see hardly anything, meager moonlight lighting the office. The black water, now level with their floor, rapidly covers the carpet. Within moments, this place will be flooded.

"The upper floor!" shouts a middle-aged woman, and she splashes across the room towards the door. The others don't need telling twice. Haruki pulls out the food he's been saving in his desk chair and shoves it into his bag. He doesn't protest when Chisa grabs his sleeve, and together they run across the office, grimacing as the water seeps through their socks. Some of the others have taken off theirs, holding them above their heads as they splash through the icy water to find the stairs.

The stairwell is pitch black, no windows giving it light. The panicking crowd engulfs him, bodies pressing together as they force themselves upwards and away from death. Someone shoves hard into Haruki, almost throwing him down the stairs.

"Calm down!" he bellows, and they stop. "Someone's going to end up breaking their neck."

"Right," says Mr. Nakamura's deep voice, somewhere to Haruki's left. "Slowly, now. Panicking isn't something we do. Hold onto someone or a banister."

It feels strangely like being in school, holding hands with the person next to them and following instructions. Haruki holds awkwardly onto his things, his backpack pressing against his belly, Chisa's cold fingers around his arm. They climb the stairs in the dark with difficulty, listening to their quick breathing and the shuffling of feet. It feels like a lifetime before they finally find the door to the floor above and push through it.

"Shouldn't we go higher?" someone suggests.

"Do you want to go through that stairwell again?" snaps a man. "No, we'll see what's here first. Maybe those three people we saw fall into the water were from this floor."

"If they are," says someone, "what were they running from?"

They fall into silence as they enter the office. It's identical to the one below, except it's much neater, no desks overturned and the glass windows intact. The now familiar smell of body odor and old socks hits them as they step inside.

"All right, spread out," mutters Mr. Nakamura. "See what you can find—"

"Who's there?"

Chisa jumps violently at the raspy voice. The window blinds are open, casting moonlight onto a shadowy figure of a man beside some boxes piled high. He was standing still, and they didn't spot him until he spoke. Their short adventure in the stairwell has adjusted Haruki's eyesight, and he can make out a man of about forty, with a matted beard and wearing a business suit that is torn and ragged.

"The lower floor is flooding," says Haruki when no one else speaks. He steps forward, looking around. He seems to be the only one here. "I'm Haruki Sato. What's your name?"

"M-Minamoto." The man fidgets, like a child who's been caught in a lie. "How many of you are there?"

"Fourteen." Mr. Nakamura steps forward. "Nice to see you again, Mr. Minamoto. We've worked together before, maybe you remember?"

It feels odd to talk about work, to remember the people Haruki has been surviving and sleeping and peeing with used to be mere coworkers.

"F-fourteen?" Minamoto doesn't seem to even notice Mr. Nakamura's greeting. "Right… I suppose you can stay…"

"Like he has a choice," someone mutters, and Haruki can't help but agree. They snooze or sit in silence until morning, some too scared to sleep, expecting the water to reach their floor in no time.

"What happens if we run out of floors to escape to?" Chisa whispers.

Haruki doesn't have an answer for that. It's too horrible a thought to consider.

Sunrise finally comes, bringing with it the usual stifling heat. Haruki glances outside to see the water still around the floor below. An odd pang runs through him at knowing their office is now lost to the depths.

Minamoto keeps to himself, often ignoring questions or giving vague answers. The others keep their distance, though they are eyeing the boxes piled in the corner.

Haruki checks his supplies. He still has a few bottles of water and several packet meals. No one thought to grab the gas cooker during their swift departure, but Chisa asks Minamoto, who points her towards one in the corner.

"Thank goodness," she says with relief as she places it on a desk in the middle of the office. "At least we'll have hot food."

They look around the office, where they find filing cabinets full of blank paper, pens, and spare furniture. This includes pillows, which they pass around with delight. Minamoto doesn't talk to anybody, sitting staring into space. Sometimes he reads a business book, but Haruki never sees him turning a page.

Something nags at Haruki whenever he glances at the quiet older man. One hot afternoon, when the sun is shining directly into the office and making everyone cranky, Haruki approaches Minamoto.

"Those three who fell into the water. They were from this office."

He doesn't frame it as a question, wondering if Minamoto will deny it. Instead, the office worker tries to push past Haruki.

"One moment." Haruki puts his hand on the wall, blocking the older man in. There's something not right about how the three office workers leaped into the water that day. Haruki wants answers. Like why they all jumped in without any sort of raft or boat. "Well?"

"They wanted to see their families," Minamoto mutters.

"But why? Surely, they saw what happened to our boss?"

Minamoto gives a strange little spasm, a shrug, perhaps. "They didn't care. Maybe they were driven insane by the conditions and the stress. Maybe they saw death as more favorable than staying here."

Haruki grimaces as he goes back to Chisa, not taking his eyes off the strange man. "I don't trust him," he whispers.

"What do we do?" she murmurs back.

Haruki looks around at where his coworkers—co *survivors*—are lying or sitting on blankets, surrounded by meager possessions they managed to bring upstairs. One of the men from the lower floor is idly sketching. Two women sit together, heads bent over a book. Tempting possibilities run through Haruki's mind: asking Minamoto to go upstairs, talking to the others about his suspicions. But if he shuns a man out simply because he is upstairs alone, what would that make him?

"We'll keep an eye on him."

Haruki doesn't say aloud his misgivings about Minamoto— that he might have forced the other three out into the water. The last thing they need now is suspicion and speculation among their group. Things are fragile enough.

"When will this ever end?" Chisa sighs as she lies on the carpet underneath a desk opposite Haruki. He looks past her at the boxes piled against the wall, wondering how many of them are from the strange drones and how much food Minamoto is keeping to himself.

Haruki closes his eyes, hugging his backpack to his chest as he listens to the low voices and slow breathing around him. Let that be a problem for tomorrow.

◆　◆　◆

Andrea is keeping watch outside the tents. She shivers, hating this job, but it's her turn. She turns over the gun in her hands. Gillian told her in private that she only has three bullets left, not that Andrea plans on using it.

It's a still night. Andrea wraps the blanket tighter around her, waiting around for midnight so she can wake up Lindsay's boyfriend Dave and change shifts. She rises to her feet and stretches, looking around. This forest in the mountains is starting to feel a little like home, they've been here so long. It's been nearly eighty days since the Rise, as people are calling it, began. People have come and gone, some to trade, others to move on after seeing the groups have occupied this side of the forest.

Andrea tucks the gun into her jeans and climbs a tree, pushing aside leaves and branches until she has a view of the town. The moonlight reflects off the black water, the town still underwater. She sighs. Her life in Boulder almost seems like a far-off dream now. Have they always been here, hiding in the woods and living on canned food, showers, and Wi-Fi a distant memory of another life?

She clambers down the tree, waving away an insect buzzing around her head, and turns to approach the camp.

A sharp gasp, a ragged inhale, as her heart jumps to her throat. A man's silhouette is there, standing between her and the others. Her hand flies to her chest, her heart threatening to burst from it.

"Whoa! Andrea, relax. It's me," says Liam, stepping towards her.

"Jesus Christ, Liam! Why are you sneaking up on me in the dark?"

"There's no need to take the Lord's name in vain," Liam scolds, stepping closer to her. He gives a small chuckle. "You need a husband, Andrea. To protect you. To lead you."

"What are you talking about?" Andrea is panting, annoyed at herself and at Liam for spooking her. "Excuse me, Liam. I need to be getting back."

"What's the rush?" As Liam comes forward, Andrea thinks she sees shapes moving in the trees. Or maybe it's her own terror making her see things. Liam is uncomfortably close. She can smell the sweat on his clothes, his cheap hair gel. She backs against the tree and his hand leans against it, blocking her in. "Do you want to hang out a bit? I've waited long enough."

"No, Liam, I don't." Andrea forces her voice not to shake. "I'm keeping watch for the camp."

"All the way over here?" Even in the darkness, Andrea can see the mocking smirk, and anger clashes with her fear. "Don't worry, *Andy*. We got it covered."

Something definitely shifts between the trees. Andrea feels like her insides have turned to water. Her knees shake, trembling as she leans against the hard trunk of the tree.

"I really like you," Liam whispers. "I changed my shifts at the movie theater to Wednesdays because that's when you usually came in. For the discount, right?"

"Liam, please stop," Andrea begs. "There's someone in the trees."

"Don't worry about them."

Fresh terror spikes through her as he leans in close. His hand takes her waist, fingers caressing the space at the bottom of her ribcage. His stale breath is warm on her ear. "I always liked Latina girls. You can be my little Spanish kitten, how about that?"

"Oh God. You're gross!" Andrea snaps, and she shoves him as hard as she can. It doesn't push him over, but his hand slips from the tree as he stumbles back.

"Bitch," he snarls. He calls over his shoulder. "Hey! I caught this woman stealing!"

"What?" Andrea gasps as men and women emerge from the trees, holding weapons and staring at her. "I didn't! He's lying!"

"Then why did you have this?" Liam holds up a can of food, flashing her a smile. He adds in a low voice, "I gave you a chance, Andrea."

"Stop this! Help!" Andrea cries as the people advance, blocking the way to the camp. She backs away, twigs and leaves snapping beneath her sneakers, her pulse racing. There are six or seven of them, all holding blunt weapons. No guns.

Gun.

Trembling, Andrea pulls out Gillian's pistol from the back of her jeans and points it shakily at Liam. "Get the fuck away from me."

For a moment, shock ripples across Liam's face. Then he laughs. "Are you going to shoot me, Andrea?"

"I will if you come any closer!" Andrea's vision tunnels as she points the gun at random people, tears burning her eyes, her breath coming in ragged gasps. The people don't advance, but they don't back away, either. "I mean it! Get away from me!"

Liam does something Andrea does not expect. He marches forward and grabs the gun, holding it to his forehead.

"Go on, Andrea." His voice is soft. "If you're going to shoot me, do it."

Andrea's lip trembles as Liam holds the pistol against his head, grinning like a madman, daring Andrea to do the unthinkable. Her finger is against the trigger, but even in the face of danger, she can't bring herself to do it. She can't shoot a man in the head. She isn't a murderer.

"Fuck," she whispers, a hot tear sliding down her cheek.

"That's what I thought." Liam tugs the gun out of her grip and tosses it to the side. The pistol glints in the moonlight as it sails over her attackers' heads and lands with a thump out of sight. "Get her."

Andrea screams and tries to run, but they are on her in seconds. Hands grab her and lift her into the air. A cold hand clamps over her mouth, muffling her screams. She looks back at the campsite. Surely they can hear her?

She screams against the palm as rough hands clutch her legs and her arms, holding her tight. Liam grins down at her. "You know what happens to those who deceive and deprive their neighbor?" he says. "They get cast into the black water."

◆　◆　◆

When Captain Spencer readied the ship to carry the passengers and crew on their Caribbean journey, the last thing he could have imagined was playing a demented game of cat and mouse. The group of passengers is angry and relentless, and there are only so many places he and Lee can hide.

"Security, what's the situation?" Captain Spencer murmurs into his walkie-talkie. His legs and back are uncomfortably stiff. Lee shivers beside him. The engine room is dark and smells of iron and rust, but at least the others haven't found them yet.

The walkie-talkie crackles. "We're prioritizing protecting the women and the families with children, sir. Where are you?"

"Are things calming down?"

"No. They're out of control, sir. Complete chaos. We have a few injured members of security. Only me and Dylan and Luka are still standing, sir."

"Understood." Captain Spencer closes his eyes as he hears Lee whimper beside him. "Robert, listen to me. Get yourselves some food and find a cabin to hide in. I don't want anyone else getting hurt."

"Roger that, sir."

"Focus on patching up the others."

The door to the engine room swings open, banging hard against the metal wall. "They've got to be in here."

"Captain!" Lee whispers, clutching Captain Spencer's jacket.

"You go ahead," he whispers to her. They'll be upon them in moments. "Let them concentrate on me."

"I'm not leaving you!" says Lee. Captain shakes his head, tears burning his eyes. Lee is foolish for not saving herself, but he's glad she is with him.

"There you are!" shouts a heavy-set man, sauntering towards them from the corner, blocking the only exit. Captain Spencer grimaces and gains his feet, holding Lee's hand.

"Thought you could boss us around just because you have a fancy hat and uniform, huh, *Captain*?" snarls a pug-faced thug, appearing on the other side. Men grab him and Lee. Lee screams, punching and kicking and biting. A man swears and slaps her across the cheek.

"Leave her alone!"

"Shut up, old man!"

Rough hands seize his arms and they drag them towards the door and into the warm summer air. It's nearly dawn, the sky orange and yellow. The sound of waves lap against the side of the ship and some seagulls caw in the distance. Under different circumstances, this would be a beautiful, pleasant morning. The men drag Captain Spencer along the deck, not caring as he stumbles. His stomach is empty, his legs sore from hiding, and despair fills him. He thinks of his wife, who he disappointed with his gambling habit yet again. Is she even still alive?

Lee struggles behind him, swearing and snarling like a cornered she-wolf. One of the thugs hits her and she groans.

"You're monsters," he murmurs, but they're making too much noise to hear him. People back out of their way as they drag them along the deck towards the fore of the ship.

"What are you doing? Stop!" roars a security team member. The mob descends on him at once.

"Run, Dylan!" the captain shouts. He doesn't want anyone to die because of him. "Get to a cabin... find Robert..."

"The ship is ours," snarls the mob leader, spittle landing on Captain Spencer's cheek. "We're not listening to your orders any—"

"Look!" Lee shouts thickly, sporting a bloody nose. "Look at the water!"

A dozen pairs of eyes look out at the sea. In the rising sunlight, they can see the water is no longer black. It has returned to a dark blue. The orange sun on the horizon is like the hopeful shining light of God. It steals Captain Spencer's breath away as it bathes his face in warmth.

"The city." Lee sobs. "Look at the city."

A day ago, Miami was mostly underwater, only the tops of the taller buildings visible. But even as they watch, the water is receding. More and more of the city becomes visible, the water disappearing. The waves beneath the cruise ship roll and rock, and the captain tugs his arms out of the mob's grip as they stare in shock at the receding water. He takes Lee's hand and they slowly back away from their attackers.

"Crew, get the lifeboats going!" Captain Spencer calls into his walkie-talkie with renewed enthusiasm and authority. He doesn't know who is still alive, who is fit for work, but they only need a few people. He, like everyone else on this wretched ship, just wants to be back on dry land and find out what happened. "Ready them all! Let's get these people back to shore!"

Lee runs off to organize the lifeboats as Captain Spencer retreats to his office, locking the door behind him. It's not until he's alone that he breaks down. He sobs, knowing that his and Lee's lives were about to end. Eighty days they have been stuck on this ship. Is that all it takes to turn average people into animals? Into murderers?

Shrill whistles pierce the air and Captain Spencer can hear his crewmates shouting to organize people. He watches out of his window as people emerge from cabins and stand near the taffrail, seeing for themselves if the water is finally going away. People laugh and cry, embracing each other or lifting children onto their shoulders so they can see. Captain Spencer shivers, not trusting any of them.

The sun has risen into the sky, sunbeams shining through the clouds, by the time most of the lifeboats have left, heading for the port. Captain Spencer stays in his office, his arms folded across his chest. He doesn't want to ride in a boat with any of those people. How many of them threw people overboard, stole food, or worse?

"Captain." Lee knocks on his door, calling softly through the wood. "Dylan and Robert have a boat ready for us, sir."

She looks awful, purple and black bruises forming by her eye, dried blood crusting on her upper lip. But she gives him a broad smile as they head for a nearby lifeboat.

It's wonderful to see the members of his trusted crew, a little worse for wear but safe and hale. He watches as a crew member lets down the latest of the lifeboats. A curly-haired teenage girl looks out at them all.

She waves to Lee. "Thank you for everything."

"Take care." Lee waves back, smiling even though she must be in a lot of pain. When the boat has gone, Captain Spencer climbs into his own, exhausted and confused. The past eighty days have been a nightmare. Who is alive back in Miami? Did things go just as crazy there, or did people find a way to coexist without resorting to violence?

He looks up at the cloudy sky as the lifeboat engine roars to life and they cut through the now-blue water towards the port. One thing is for sure. He'll never gamble again.

◆　◆　◆

Haruki awakens to shouting, and jumps awake, getting tangled in his thin blanket. Minamoto and Mr. Nakamura are engaged in a fight, Mr. Nakamura holding the middle-aged man in a headlock.

"What's going on?" roars Haruki.

"This little weasel needs to share his food!" Mr. Nakamura wheezes. The young man's face grows steadily more purple.

"You're choking him!"

"Serves him right!"

Someone slams into them both, pulling at the young man's sweat-soaked shirt. Murakami wriggles free, massaging his throat.

"You killed those three workers, didn't you?" Mr. Nakamura bellows. He's red in the face himself, panting from exhaustion. "They didn't jump on purpose. You forced them out!"

Minamoto straightens, and quick as a flash, pulls out a penknife. He flicks it and the blade gleams in the daylight. "Touch me again and you're dead," he snarls, his voice raspy. "Yes, I forced those three out. They were getting greedy. But when it came down to it, they were cowards. I'm the one who's survived. You're not taking my food! I've worked too hard for it!"

Minamoto doesn't notice the bespectacled man from downstairs sneaking up behind him. Haruki's heart jumps to his throat as he leaps onto his back, yanking him backwards. Mr. Nakamura darts forward to wrestle the knife from his hands.

Others run in, joining the fray. Haruki backs away, watching the office workers as they finally snap. Chisa manages to break free of the bizarre group brawl and collapses against the wall beside him, breathing hard.

"What's happening to us?" she moans. "Someone's going to be killed!"

Haruki darts for the boxes against the wall and yanks one open. There isn't much inside, a couple of breakfast bars and some packets of instant food, but to a starving man, anything looks like heaven.

Is this what eighty days of hardship does to people? Were they all just waiting for a catalyst to snap? Is this the true nature of mankind that has just been stifled by modern laws and frivolous distractions?

Some of the people, like Mrs. Yamada, are staying out of the fight, watching in horror, or looking around, perhaps wondering whether to try and go upstairs. People yell and fight, cloth tearing. Someone yelps in pain. Haruki can't tear his eyes off the animalistic display. He expects to see blood any second.

One woman looks outside the window and shouts something.

"Stop it, everyone! Stop!" she bellows, pointing at the window. One by one, people join her. "The water!"

Haruki runs to the glass and peers out.

The water is receding. Going from black to blueish gray, the level is lowering, like someone has just pulled the plug in an enormous bathtub. The fighting slowly ends, people rubbing bruised limbs or massaging sore jaws as they look outside. People start moving around the windows in the buildings around. Someone across the street cheers.

Haruki doesn't believe it. He doesn't dare to.

"Give me that," snaps Mrs. Yamada, of all people, and wrenches the knife from Minamoto's hands as he stares dumbly out of the window. The knife sails outside and lands in the lowering water with a splash.

"You won't get away with what you did, I'll see to that" says Mr. Nakamura. Minamoto blanches, his lip quivering, as he backs away from them. Then he darts for the door and crashes out of it, his footsteps echoing on the stairwell. Nobody tries to follow him.

"Haruki," whispers Chisa as he sits against the wall, sighing as he closes his eyes. It's a dream. In a minute, they'll all wake up for another monotonous day. "Haruki, I think... I think it's over."

"Is it?" he asks weakly, looking up to meet her eyes. The thought of things returning to normal, to being able to walk the streets, see his family, eat whatever he wants, take a shower... no, it must all be an old dream. Too good to be true.

◆　◆　◆

The sky flashes with lightning, a torrent of rain falling from the heavens. Andrea gave up trying to struggle out of the mob's arms, but the rain makes them gasp and splutter, their grips slipping. A bolt of lightning burns across her vision and the rain soaks her to the skin. Gasping, Andrea twists, trying to writhe out of the attackers' tight fists.

Agony explodes across her temple as someone punches her. "Stay still, bitch!"

The storm rages on, a cacophony of mayhem rattling her skull. They carry her, like some weird offering, towards the black water. How close are they to it? Will she drown or be struck by lightning?

She breathes slow, saving her energy. Fists grip her soaking sweater, another hand tightly closed around her thigh with bruising pressure. The group stumbles through the forest, feet squelching on mud, jumping at the cracking thunder rumbling through the mountainside.

Andrea counts to ten, feeling her heartbeat slow in her ribcage. One twist, one lucky break, and she can make a run for it. She refuses to let these disgusting men kill her. She didn't survive this long to be drowned.

Nine... ten!

Andrea twists hard, lashing out with her foot. She lands a kick on something hard and hears a howl of pain as she falls painfully to the ground, the mud beneath her slick and sticking to her. Confusion reigns as people yell and try to navigate through the darkness. Andrea crawls, gasping, half blind in the rainy night, as boots rush around her. Someone trips over her and goes sprawling to the ground. A pained yell. Andrea drags herself along and grabs at the grass, then scrambles to her feet and runs.

She sobs as she stumbles along, slipping on the thick mud. She was so close to being killed. She throws a look behind her as bright flashes of lightning illuminates the forest. Rain falls, soaking people fighting and shouting. Andrea runs, not knowing which way the campsite is, wishing she had the gun.

But it'll be ruined with water damage by now even if she does find it.

They must leave, get out of here.

The thunderstorm stops as quickly as it started, and for a moment it feels like it happened just so Andrea could get away. That's ridiculous, of course.

Panting hard, Andrea pushes her way into some thick trees, hoping to shake off her pursuers. Once they've recovered and realized she's gone, they'll no doubt come back. She listens, hearing the water fall from the trees and the wind howl in the mountains, but there's no sign of Liam and the others.

How she manages to find the campsite, she has no idea. Maybe a subconscious part of her memorized this part of the forest. She stumbles to the tent, where Gillian and Lindsay are outside and looking around.

"Andrea! Oh God, what happened? We woke up because of the storm and you weren't here…"

"We've got to go," Andrea pants. "Come on, let's go. Liam attacked me… he's got other people… they're coming!"

Lindsay gapes at her, but a hard expression crosses Gillian's face. "Right you are, Andrea. Come on, everybody, let's pack away the tents."

"There's no time!" Andrea looks behind her, terrified she'll see the attackers emerging from the tree line to kill them all. "We need to go right now."

"Where's my gun?"

Andrea swallows. "I'm sorry, Gillian. They took it…"

"It's okay." Gillian gives her a small smile. "Jackson, honey, let's get up."

Andrea can't relax until they've thrown the essentials into their cars and have come out onto the road. Andrea is in the back of Lindsay's car, letting the Knights drive hers. The sun is rising, the taste of dawn on the horizon as the birds start to chirp. A couple of trees are lying on their sides, destroyed by the freak thunderstorm.

Lindsay curses as men run onto the road, blocking their escape. Andrea gives a low moan. In the gathering dawn, they're even more frightening, covered in mud and murder in their eyes.

Liam wanders in front of the car, his dark hair a tousled mess, a smug smile on his face. "Nice try, my love, but no one can escape the will of God. Andrea tried to steal from us and she must be punished. Hand her over, and we'll let you go."

"I didn't steal anything!"

"Of course you didn't. He's a psycho," Lindsay growls. Her dark hands tighten on the steering wheel.

"Give her to us *now* or we're slashing your tires." Liam holds up a knife.

"Screw that." Lindsay revs the engine. "Get out of the way or I'll run you over!"

Liam laughs, a terrible sound void of warmth. "You don't have the—"

The car lurches forward with a roar.

WHAM.

"Oh my God!" Andrea buries her face in her hands as Liam is thrown to the side of the road with the most horrendous banging sound Andrea has ever heard.

Dave is sitting bolt upright in his seat, his mouth open in shock. Liam's cronies run from the road as they trundle along, Andrea's car right behind theirs. Lindsay is breathing hard, shifting gears as she glances in the rear-view mirror. Andrea doesn't dare look.

"Where will we go now?" she says instead. Her voice sounds so weak and tired. The sun rises over a mountain, casting warm light on the earth. Several birds fly up to the blue sky, clearer than Andrea has seen it in months.

"We…" Lindsay's voice fades away as she gasps, stopping the car.

"What? What?" Andrea looks around, expecting to see more attackers.

"Look!"

Andrea leans forward, pushing herself between Lindsay and her boyfriend. Boulder sits before them like a photograph, nestled in the valley, and…

The water. "It's gone."

They sit in silence, unable to take in what they are seeing. The horrible black water, rising higher every day, has disappeared. The town sits as normal before them, except the roads are voice of cars and people. The scene could be a postcard in a drugstore.

"It's over!" says Dave. He grins at them both. His eyes are bloodshot, his face gaunt, but he's wearing the only smile Andrea has seen since he and Lindsay arrived in the mountains. "It's over!"

◆　◆　◆

Stephanie looks out of the window of the lifeboat to where Miami awaits. It's almost strange to see the city out of the water. It was underwater for so long she forgot how big it was.

The water, somehow, receded overnight. Callum sits with his hands against another window, looking out at the water. It is no longer black, and as Stephanie glances over, a little fish darts past. Things are finally returning to normal.

Dad sits on the other side, staring straight ahead. Mom has her eyes closed, whispering something beneath her breath. Sadness and anxiety steal over Stephanie. Even though the rise is over, the world will never be the same again. Their home will be a sodden, rotting mess. Millions will be dead or homeless. Will the adults be able to rebuild a life worth living, or were the events on the cruise ship only a taste of what's to come?

A helicopter flies overhead and Stephanie watches it for as long as she can before it disappears, the lifeboat's roof hindering her view.

Everyone gasps as the familiar rhythmic pulses rock the lifeboats. Callum screams and buries his face in Mom's lap. A voice, robotic and monotone, rumbles through the boat.

"We are now among you,"

"Be better. Do better."

THE END

Printed in Great Britain
by Amazon

24840700R00071